Keeper'sBook™

FROM THE EDITORS OF KEEPERS AT HOME MAGAZINE

Protecting
their
Purity

Protecting innocent children from sexual abuse
Stories and how-to for mothers

Keeper'sBook™ series focuses on specific topics relevant to *Keepers at Home* readers. Our goal is to bring together talented writers who have passion for the subject and readers whose lives will be blessed by the information presented in each Keeper'sBook™.

ISBN: 978-1-933753-67-6

Cover Design: Veritas Creative
Text Design: Larisa Yoder

2673 Township Road 421
Sugarcreek, OH 44681
1-800-852-4482
Fax: 330-852-3285

Carlisle Press
WALNUT CREEK

Foreword

We used to sweep it under the cultural carpet of ignorance, denial, pride, and the it's-the-way-things-are mindset. It happens a lot, get over it was often the medieval era medicine we offered to victims.

Sexual abuse.

At times we have the audacity to blame the world. It's true, the world's offerings on moral purity offer no hope—only despair. Their slide into depravity and its awful consequences provides an unsolvable problem for them.

But we can't blame the world. Sexual abuse among plain people is *our* problem. It's the parents' problem. It's the church's problem. It's a problem of the unregenerated heart. And like any other problem of the heart the Bible has the answers.

And not only is it *our* problem—it's *our* responsibility. With *Protecting Their Purity* our objective is to raise the standard—sexual abuse is not normal. It's not right. It must stop. It must end.

I know, many of our readers may struggle with talking about the details of something so private—so sacred—in print. For anyone to read. I empathize.

But this problem won't go away if men and women don't take a long, hard look at root causes and biblical solutions—if we don't stand up and tell each other this behavior is sin. It must stop. God wants parents and church leaders who will speak out. Speak up. And who won't shut up until we have made every effort to stop sexual abuse. We realize that *Protecting Their Purity* will not answer all the questions. Fix all the problems. End all the abuse.

We are however raising a significant voice against it. And along with you we want to ask God to show us what we can do individually and collectively to be clear before God in this matter. The sinful activity must end, but more importantly, the heart conditions that lead to this sin must change. As a people group we must return to belief in the power of Jesus Christ to transform the human heart into something different. Something new. Something pure. A heart of love that abhors abuse. A heart of love that reaches to those suffering from the effects of it. A heart so full of love for God that this great evil becomes ever increasingly evil until we finally think like God does about it.

So help us, God.

Marvin Wengerd

Table of Contents

Dear Daughter

Berneice Leid

Dear Daughter,

For this child I prayed…Not many years ago, you were my darling little girl, charmingly inquisitive, bursting with sunshine and sweetness. How I loved you then and prayed I could be all you needed, to gently guide those innocent feet in paths of light and love. With remarkable swiftness those years have passed and today you stand, with me at your side, at the threshold of beautiful womanhood. Though thought impossible, my mother love has grown as you have grown. As you teeter on the edge, ready to try your wings, my prayers follow you. Today I pray I could point the way, protect from pitfalls the enemy would wile against you. As I listen to your prayers to your Saviour, I see a young woman with convictions and dreams. How earnestly I long to be able to shield you and keep that precious innocence, lest it become marred. I pray you could adopt values of purity and chastity. This world has glitz and glamour, and its boasting is not shy. But a young woman who fears the Lord prays for wisdom. As you grow in maturity and knowledge you will observe the world around you. You will see examples of womanhood cheaply displayed. But I long for my dear daughter a more excellent way. A way of modesty and moral honor. There will be the temptation to flirt or behave boldly in dress or conduct. But a young woman who fears the Lord will not seek to expose or reveal. Her womanhood is covered respectfully and reservedly for the one man who will become her husband. Please understand when I warn against immodesty, it is not to restrict you but to liberate you, to protect you from negative attention. Because, as you see, immodest dress and actions will definitely attract attention, but it is not the attention you think. Decency attracts decency. A young woman who fears the Lord takes life seriously, realizing all actions have consequences. One cannot play with fire and not be burned. Please remember you are given only one life to live and one can never go back. As a mother I have been given the responsibility of leading, you and there is no better time to live for the Lord than in your youth. You may think modesty issues belong to the worldly folks we see so blatantly displayed. But dear daughter, it concerns you directly as you learn to sew and join your friends. I challenge you to be an example and inspiration to the people around you. It is my most earnest desire for you to have lived a life of no regrets, a life of zeal and love for the Lord. A young woman who fears the Lord can be whole in spirit, soul, and body.

Your loving mother

Where
Are the Mothers?

Anonymous

"Where Are the Mothers" shows sexual abuse in three different settings. But one thing is constant—missing parental involvement. These three stories are true though names have been changed.

Six-year-old Amanda gently rocked back and forth in her little rocker and hummed a little tune to the dolly in her arms. When the "baby" started crying she tenderly lifted it to her shoulder and patted her back. "Are you hungry, baby dear?" she crooned. Digging around in a diaper bag for a bottle, she changed her mind and opted to "breastfeed" her instead. Pretending to open her dress, she held the little dolly against herself and started humming again.

Yes, Amanda was learning all about babies. Hadn't her mother just brought a new baby home from the hospital about a month ago? How thrilled she was with the new bundle and how eagerly she absorbed all about the care and feeding of the baby as little girls will. It was all so new and exciting to her and now her own dollies were receiving excellent care too.

Marlene, four years older than Amanda, entered the bedroom with two of her own dolls in her arms. "I have twins today," she announced. Amanda smiled. Marlene knew so much more than she did. Hadn't she told her that the new baby had not actually come from the hospital, but that it was made and grew in Mother's belly? "What else does she know that she isn't telling?" Amanda wondered as she continued rocking her baby.

Several hours later the two girls were still playing with their dolls in their bedroom. Amanda wandered downstairs, into the kitchen and living room, looking for her mother. Even as she looked, she knew that she would not find her. "Working out in the store again," she thought with a lonely feeling. At least she had Marlene with her. When she went back to the bedroom Marlene had a pillow under her dress. "Look," she said. "My baby isn't born yet." She joined her hands under the pillow, showing off a well-rounded "belly." "I'm pregnant. Did you know that that is the word for a mother that is going to have a baby?" When Amanda giggled and shook her head, Marlene asked, "Do you want to try it too?" So the two girls continued their play until Mother came in from the store to make dinner.

The next day they were alone again; this time they were practicing having their babies born. "We go to the closet when the babies are born," informed Marlene. "That way if someone comes in they won't see us." After several hours alone again, the two girls became bored once more. Sitting side by side in the bedroom, Marlene whispered, "Do you know how the babies get into the bellies?" When Amanda simply shook her head Marlene once again headed for the closet. "I will show you, but remember, we have to hide when we do this, okay?" She paused when Amanda nodded, then continued, "First we have to take off our underwear, the same as we do when the babies are born. Then I will pretend that I am the dad. It always takes a mom and a dad."

Where Marlene got her information at ten years of age, we may never know. But we do know that the two girls continued to play making babies day after day while their mother was working in the store, leaving them alone for hours at a time. Little Amanda lost not only her innocence but became sexually aroused at the tender age of six years old. Even though she was a very hesitant participant at the beginning and felt a dreadful sense of wrong and shame with their type of play, she had trusted her older sister up until then and did not think that she would do anything very bad to her. The two girls were often lonely with Mother working so much and learned that the good feelings that went with their play helped to make the loneliness better. She had no reason to feel any fear for what they were doing.

Later, one day when Marlene was not at home and Amanda was feeling particularly lonely, she went to the closet alone, wishing that she had her sister to do the "feel good things" with. That day, hiding there in the closet, she learned that this is something you can do alone. She had no way of knowing that what she learned that day would become a habit long before she ever reached puberty. All she knew was that it felt good and that you have to hide while it is done because it is a shameful thing. Soon she learned that when she felt particularly sad or lonely, when things were stressful in her home, when Mother was cross, or the baby cried, that she could go to the closet and do this thing that would make her feel momentarily better.

She had no way of knowing that by the time she reached puberty there would be many places to hide to do this besides the closet, and that she would use increasingly more impure things to help with the habit.

She had no way of knowing that being used "that way" as a little girl, and being so sexually overstimulated at such a young age would set her up for another, much more invasive and damaging sexual abuse incident later, a situation where she felt even more powerlessness and betrayal than she had felt with her sister.

She had no way of knowing that by the time she was ready for marriage the "habit" would be a daily thing. Or that after all that time of going to her habit to help her cope with any negative feelings, she would therefore not be satisfied with what marriage had to offer.

She had no way of knowing that when she finally did realize that what she was doing was sinful that she would struggle for many years to overcome the habit. After all, something that was done for 15 years is not easily stopped. Her body was addicted.

She had no way of knowing that because of what was done to her as a little girl, she would struggle through years and years of tremendous pain in her marriage relationship, struggle with feelings of worthlessness, shame, guilt, mistrust, and loss.

She did not know that what she had experienced was indeed called sexual abuse because of what it did to her. She always thought it wouldn't be called abuse because it was done by a girl.

All this pain and damage was done to this little girl, this teenager, and this adult, because a mother thought it is okay to leave two little girls alone for many hours while she was working in her store.

Where are the mothers? Do mothers realize that even if it is only two girls, even then they need your protection and supervision. And the way to protect your children is to know where they are and what they are doing at all times. Yes, even if it is only girls.

∞∞∞

Malinda was so excited! Today they were going to Aunt Jane's house. At five years old, she looked forward to going away with Mother and today was extra special. She bounced up and down on the back seat of the van in eager anticipation. "Keep still until I have your shoes on," her mother told her. "Next time we'll put them on before you leave the house." She was smiling as she talked, and Malinda could feel that Mother was also looking forward to their day. She didn't get to be with her sisters as often as she liked and today they were going to be doing one of her favorite hobbies, scrap-booking and making cards together.

But that was not what Malinda cared about. What she was most excited about was the fact that Aunt Jane lived on a farm and she would get to see all the animals and play with her cousins besides.

When they finally arrived Malinda ran into the house and looked for her cousins. What a disappointment for both Malinda and her mother that one of her aunts wasn't able to come after all, which meant that her three little girl cousins weren't there either. That left her with only Aunt Jane's son Richard to play with. Even though he was six years older than she was, she soon found herself tagging after him as he showed her all the animals in the barn. How scared she felt when she saw the long row of cows with their big eyes! She was glad when Richard offered to take her to see the new puppies instead. They had fun playing with them in the haymow and after they grew tired of that they watched the chickens peck around in their yard. "Do you want to throw in some feed for them?" asked Richard.

"Yes!" Her eyes shone as she clutched handfuls of feed and threw it into the pen where the chickens pecked hungrily in the dirt. "This is so much fun!" she said. How she wished that she lived on a farm too.

A yummy lunch was eaten while animated talking and gabbing went on among the aunts. They went from eating to doing dishes without pause in the laughter, stories, and bits of gossip. Richard and Malinda sat on the couch looking at books. His story finished, he leaned towards Malinda. "Do you want to go see the puppies again?" he asked. Her eyes took in the messy table full of scrap-booking supplies and the aunts doing the dishes. She slipped off the couch and went to her mother's side.

"Mom, may we go out and see the puppies again?" she asked. Her mother barely paused in her conversation to give Malinda a nod of her head, then went on with her story.

So the two cousins found themselves playing with the puppies in the barn again while the patient momma dog looked on. Soon they took another walk to see all the other animals, then found themselves back with the puppies again. As the afternoon wore on Malinda found herself getting sleepy from the day's excitement and stretched out in the hay, hands on her chin, watching the puppies play. Richard stretched out beside her and they felt a special closeness, a seclusion from the rest of the world.

"We could pretend that we are animals too," said Richard. "Did you know that mommy and daddy animals get on top of each other like this?" he demonstrated.

Malinda was quite hesitant at first. Something seemed wrong with what they were doing. But Richard had been so kind and caring all day and she could see no reason to mistrust him. So she giggled and asked, "Is that what the rooster was doing when we were watching the chickens?"

"You bet he was," Richard affirmed. "And I have even seen the bull do it that we have with the heifers. You should see that; it's really something. And I saw our daddy dog do it to this momma dog too."

Malinda's eyes were round as saucers at all this information, but he seemed to be so wise and understanding that when he offered to show her again, she complied.

So they were together. Alone. No one came to check on them or to see where they were all this time. In the next half hour their innocent play was innocent no more. Animals never wore clothes, so people did not really need any either, did they? At least not when they were playing the animals game. When the mothers finally called for them they quickly ended their play and ran for the house. Mother was fondly telling her sisters goodbye and was admiring all the pretty things they had created that day. She did not notice the few tears of confusion and pain slip down her daughter's cheek on the back seat of the van, and when she saw that she had fallen asleep on the way home she only accounted it to the excitement of a day on the farm. She was so busy relating all the day's conversations to her husband that evening that she hardly noticed how quiet and withdrawn her daughter seemed all evening. She had no way of knowing that because of her neglect and lack of vigilance terrible damage was done to her daughter that day. All because of unsupervised innocent play. She had no way of knowing that when the family was together again several weeks later for a Sunday dinner that she should have special reason to be especially vigilant.

That Sunday, it was the first thing that both Malinda and Richard thought about when they looked at each other. Even though she felt like she loved him for his kind and caring ways, she dropped her head and eyes in shame and guilt. She felt so much confusion about what had actually happened the last time they were together.

There were more people there that day, but it seemed as if Richard was watching for his chance. When she found herself alone on the way to the house, Richard met her behind the garage and convinced her to play the animals game again. Feeling powerless both in size and strength, she felt as if she had no choice but to comply.

In the next five years whenever the families were together, which was fairly frequently, Richard sexually abused Malinda as often as he was able to. After she was ten years old she became shrewd enough to never get caught alone with him. Even though the abuse ended, what followed was a lifetime of having to deal with mistrust of others and God, betrayal, confusion, shame, and pain. Richard, a perpetrator at 16 years old, turned to another little girl to support his perversion. All because of what began in innocent play and lack of supervision and vigilance from his mother.

∞∞∞

"Time for bed, boys," said Mother at the close of another busy day of working in the produce fields.

"Yes, Mother," answered seven-year-old Joel. He was tired, so he put his toy tractors away then knelt down by her side for his nightly prayers. She gave him a kiss on the cheek and wished him her customary, "Sleep well." As he went up the stairs he heard his next two older brothers, Jason, age 10, and Matthew, age 14, following him.

"Lucky brothers," he thought to himself. They did everything together, even slept in the same room while he slept in a room all by himself. The thought of being alone way at the end of the hall filled him with a bit of loneliness. Everyone had been so busy today and he hadn't felt as if anyone had any time to talk with him or listen to what was important to him. Passing his 17-year-old brother Jerry's room, Joel noticed that his light was on. He had always admired Jerry and looked up to him. Didn't he usually take time to listen to him when everyone else was too busy working? So seeking a bit of companionship, he peeked in at the door. Jerry was sitting on the bed with his back turned, looking at something in his hands. When he detected movement at the door he quickly stuffed it under the bed and turned with a guilty look on his face. Seeing that it was only Joel, he relaxed and smiled.

"Howdy, little bro," he said, reaching out to tousle his hair. "What are you up to?"

"Hey Jerry, what were you looking at? May I see it too?" said Joel in answer. "Did you put it under your bed?" Joel moved quickly. More quickly than Jerry had anticipated and before he knew what had happened Joel held his pornographic magazine in his hands.

"Hey! That's not for little boys to look at," he said, grabbing to get it back. But Joel had already seen more than any boy, young or old, should ever see.

The next months were very busy summer months on the produce farm. Too young to help much with the work, and still too old to need watching all the time, Joel found himself alone a lot. In the evenings when the work was done everyone was too tired to give him much attention, and consequently he dealt with more and more feelings of loneliness and sadness.

One day soon after he had gotten a glimpse of Jerry's magazine, he was feeling especially lonely and decided to see if he could find it in his room. Sure enough, he found it under his mattress. He felt so dirty and ashamed, looking at such pictures, but still he seemed drawn to them. He was not sure what to think of all these strange new feelings surging through his body.

That evening he entered his brother's bedroom again, and before long the two boys were spending their evenings together in either one or the other of the bedrooms. Sometimes they just spent the time talking. Sometimes they looked at the magazine together. Sometimes they lay beside each other on the same bed, enjoying the closeness, both physically and emotionally.

One evening, in the semi-darkness, when they had been looking at the magazine together, Jerry introduced Joel to self-gratification. At first it seemed so shameful and wrong to Joel. But in a sense it was just a step further than looking at the magazine.

Neither of them knew quite when it happened or how it started, but one thing led to another and soon Jerry was touching not only his own body, but also Joel's. Too late, Joel knew that this was not the kind of attention he wanted. He felt so much guilt and confusion with what was happening. Very much, he wanted it to stop. One day he vowed to tell his mother what was happening, all about the magazine, and all their time spent together alone. But that day the truck farm was very busy with customers. Every time Joel went to Mother she seemed extra busy with other people. Once, when he kept following her, she told him to go play and keep out of her way.

So he left her side, a sad little broken boy, his heart bleeding and crying inside. Crying for help but not knowing where to go if his own mother did not have time for him. Too busy to really notice that her son was more and more withdrawn and struggled with outbursts of anger that were very uncharacteristic of him. Too busy to see that her son's heart was broken and his life damaged.

He stopped going to Jerry's room at night, but Jerry did not stop coming to his. What began as a happy friendship and a meeting of his emotional needs, ended as a terrible feeling of powerlessness and betrayal. The abuse continued for several more years, until Jerry left home. But the irreparable damage was done.

ooooooooooooooooooooooooooooooooooooooooooooooooooooooooooooooooooooooo

What terrible damage is done when mothers get so caught up in work or hobbies that their children are left unsupervised for hours at a time, both in the day and in the night! How terribly life-changing and devastating! How many profound losses! How much pain and damage! How many years of pain and tears! What a struggle to heal and mend! How many hours needed to spend in counseling or support groups!

Please, please, mothers, your children should be more important than any kind of work or hobby. Take the work of raising and protecting them seriously. ❀

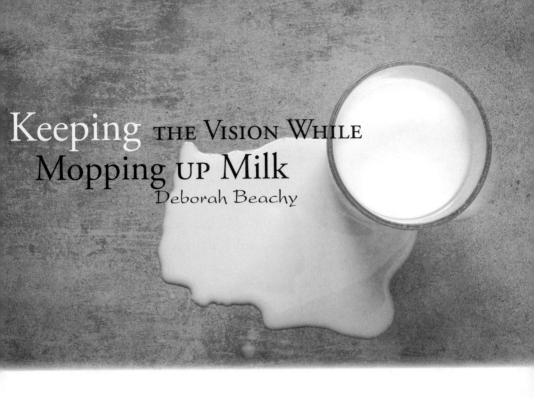

Keeping THE VISION WHILE Mopping UP Milk
Deborah Beachy

G ina pushed aside a sticky oatmeal bowl, a jelly-smeared bib, and the cricket which her son Michael had captured yesterday for a pet, but was now—dead? A thin leg moved feebly. "Michael!" hollered Gina. "Come get this creature off the breakfast table!"

Michael strolled into the kitchen. "I was feeding it grape jelly," he said as he scooped it up. " It didn't eat much—too much sugar probably."

Gina couldn't imagine her son feeding a cricket at the table without her noticing, but then, she'd been busy fishing chunks of scrambled egg out of Marcia's juice and asking Joe about his plans for the day, hoping he'd have time to fix the washing machine.

He didn't. Gina had figured this, but still…She had put on her last clean everyday dress this morning. Tomorrow? She imagined Joe's face if he came in from his barn chores and found her flapping around in a maternity dress.

"What's so funny, Mom?"

Gina jolted back to her brown-eyed son. "The jelly was sugar free," she told him. "I think the cricket is used to…bugs for breakfast." Did crickets eat bugs? Who knew?

Michael grinned cautiously. Bugs for breakfast—really? He balanced the cricket on his arm and loped out into the June sunshine.

Gina finished clearing a spot at the table, then sat down with the survey that had come in yesterday's mail. If she couldn't do laundry, she could do this. She shook open the page and read the title: *What Do Parents Desire Most for Their Children?*

Ahh. Loaded question. Gina clicked her pen. There was a long list of options:

Social popularity.

Good looks.

High IQ.

Financial stablility.

And then—

Freedom from moral restrictions.

Gina's neck prickled. How could any parent desire that for their children? She wadded the survey in a crumpled ball and threw it in the trash. The trashcan was full—she may as well get the matches and burn it right away.

Orange flames snatched at empty egg cartons and hot dog wrappers. The survey popped, curled up, and turned to gray ashes that floated away on the breeze. Gina wondered briefly whether she should have let Joe read it. But it had been humanistic. So very anti-God. Gina knew Joe would not have wanted her to waste time in getting rid of it.

Still, they talked it over. "What do *you* desire most for our children?" Joe asked.

Gina half-chuckled, half-sighed. "I thought about that today. I realized that in the noisy close-up of mothering, I get distracted by what needs to be done right now: teach these children to not hammer wildly on the bathroom door when I need just a moment's peace, to not scribble a doll's face with red permanent marker to give it a sunburn, to not talk with meatballs in their mouth..."

"That's good," Joe said. "We don't want to bring up a bunch of self-centered rogues."

"But I get stuck on those things. I mean, I obsess about the meatball hanging out of Michael's mouth when I should be thinking more about the kind of man I want him to become."

"What do you want him to become?"

"Saved, of course. Honest and dependable—a lot of things."

"I think a long-range vision for our children is important; it's also important to remember the details. The things we drill over and over today is what it takes to reach that vision." Joe grinned. "Like if we want Michael-the-man to impress his wife, we drill Michael-the-boy to hold the bear story until the meatball's down."

"And if we want Marcia-the-woman to be modest, I shouldn't let Marcia-the-two-year-old use her skirt as general transportation for her toys? Maybe if I'd start sewing huge pockets on her dresses..."

Joe tapped his foot, the way he did when he was processing. "We put in a lot of sweat teaching our children to be respectful and obedient—what about areas where the results might not stand out so much until later? Like—their purity. Do we neglect that?"

"Well, I know one thing," said Gina. "That survey rattled me! This country is going to the dogs!"

"We forget that the strength of a man is directly tied to his purity. Or we ignore it; it's easier to teach table manners."

"Will our children know how—and why—to stay pure if we're too embarrassed or too lazy to talk to them about it?"

"Not any more than they'll know it's rude to belch and eat macaronis with their fingers unless we tell them."

"There's more than one way of losing one's purity," said Gina. "You can do it willfully, or you can have it taken by force. I'm thinking of one of my friends. Some boy used to hunt her down and do all sorts of hideous stuff to her. What if that happened to Marcia? I worry sometimes."

"You're saying our children can take a stand for themselves, but if somebody else shows up, they're helpless?"

"I guess so. Yes."

Joe tapped his foot some more. "In one way you're right," he said. "If a husky fifteen-year-old dragged Marcia off somewhere, she'd have about as much chance as a mouse with a cat. But couldn't we prepare her in case that happened?"

"Like you said, table manners are easier!"

Joe swung to his feet. "Look, it's getting kind of late if I want to get up in time to fix the washing machine, but what say you talk with your friend? Ask her if she thinks easier is always better."

◦◦

I am Gina's friend. I think table manners are important, but no one's going to die if Michael belches after a big dish of bread pudding. But if Michael's purity is stolen, a big part of his heart will die.

Gina is a good mom who wants to give her children the tools they need to face life. But she wonders, as moms and dads do everywhere: are there tools to protect against child abuse?

Is abuse a threat in our plain communities?

We love to prop up our feet and take comfort in our sheltered environment. What more can happen to our snub-nosed, freckle-faced darlings than a wagon crash at the bottom of Grandpa's hill?

Of course, a wagon crash can be pretty brutal: blood dripping into dust, bruises swelling, moans coming loud. But it's nothing that some salve and a chocolate kiss from Grandma won't cure.

The bad stuff—child predators, rape, incest, fondling—that's in mainstream society, right? We can kind of turn our deck chairs away from that direction and soak up the laughter from barefoot lassies making daisy chains...

Some years ago, on a July afternoon when it seemed the whole world was baking, a little brown-haired girl wandered amongst the daisies at the edge of a garden. Every now and then she plucked off a drooping stem; soon her hands would be full and she'd put them all in a quart jar of cool water where they'd stand up straight once more.

She didn't know The Boy was sneaking up on her until she glimpsed the battered hat rustling through the corn rows. She started wildly, then let go of her daisies and the little tune she was humming all in an instant. She plunged through the garden, through the prickling cucumber vines and bushy beans and tomato plants bending low with fat red tomatoes. The Boy was loping behind her; he was laughing, a sound that filled her with terror. She knew he liked watching her run. It was part of his game. She glanced at the tall brick house under the oaks. If somebody saw her, maybe they'd stop him...or maybe think they were just playing.

She burst out of the garden, lungs choking on the hot, close air. Up ahead rose the weathered gray of the woodshed. That's where he finally grabbed her. Holding her tightly against his damp shirt, he took her inside and latched the door.

The little girl was me. What happened in the woodshed, and other places on other days, affected me for many years. I did not tell anybody until I was grown up. I thought I was alone, that such things never happened to anybody else.

I was wrong. I have since listened to dozens of other women laying bare their secrets of molestation. I have read statistics: by the age of eighteen, one in every four girls will have been molested.

It happens.

Today I am a parent. I look at my little girl and I wonder how to protect her. Should I stand guard over her in bug-eyed fear? Should I invest in a picket rope so she's never out of my sight? Or should I angle the deck chair away from the murky sea of memories and hope she'll somehow grow up safe?

I don't have all the answers. I know how abuse rips open the heart and leaves it a wind-scoured desert. I know God can grow roses in the desert. But to teach my children? I am like Gina. I would rather stress the belching rule.

We parents have a responsibility. If we dodge it, could we be watering the same root that lay at the heart of Gina's survey? *An utter lack of vision.*

Maybe that's too strong. For those of us who embrace the Word, life itself becomes a vision. Eternity is an imminent reality. We push hard the pendulum, urging our children toward conviction, purpose, and rough-hewn beams thumped down atop Calvary.

Everything matters.

It's just that sometimes the deck chairs are a little too comfortable. And we get tired in this noisy clamor of bringing up children. And would it do any good to fight? Children still get molested. Tears still streak dusty faces. Hearts still turn hard and cynical.

Twice a week, Gina takes a can of milk and a little basket of fresh eggs to the granny down the road. She uses these excursions to teach the children road safety. She talks about stop signs and traffic lights and turning signals. She stresses keeping on the right side of the road and using lights after dark. She knows there is always a certain amount of danger on a road; you can never be absolutely sure you won't have an accident. Yet by observing traffic laws and using common sense, most accidents can be avoided.

It is much the same in preserving our children's purity. We can never be guaranteed that nothing bad will happen, but with a reasonable amount of teaching and precaution, many would-be heartaches can be avoided.

Maybe it's time to rise out of the deck chairs. Time to gather the children and breathe life to the vision. Following are four areas in which to make it practical.

1. Vigilance. Being aware of what goes on in your child's life is part of your responsibility as a parent. However, there is a difference between being vigilant versus overprotective. The first is motivated by concern; the second by fear.

If you, or someone you know, has been abused, you may be quick to become overprotective. Sometimes as I watch my daughter skip and twirl with strawberry juice on her skirt and hair escaping braids, I get this little ache inside. I remember when my girlhood went dark. There is an almost desperate urge to make sure it doesn't happen to her.

I keep watch. As Gina does. As you do. How do we know if we are doing our job or if we're wild-eyed worrywarts?

Here are a few indicators that you may be overprotective:

—You're unable to leave your child with a babysitter.

—You view all people and situations with mistrust.

—You're in a state of agitation the minute your child disappears from sight.

—When you're changing your baby's diaper and another child edges too close, you get frustrated and angry.

—You can never relax and enjoy a gathering because you're too busy trying to figure out who's a threat.

You may argue that being overprotective is justified. Remember that the motivator behind overprotection is fear. God has not given us the spirit of fear. Can something that is not from God bring good results?

Tethering my daughter to a picket rope might indeed keep her from a peeping Tom—or worse—but she's going to feel stifled and unloved and will learn to resent me.

What does vigilance look like?

Let's say Gina is ready to go to Granny's with the milk and eggs. The children beg to go along because they love Granny and the little jar of corn candy she keeps in her spice cupboard. But Granny's nephew is visiting and he just recently got out of jail for child molestation. So Gina asks Joe if the children can stay with him, and Joe says the best thing is to go himself.

If the danger is real, you will not subject your children to it.

Being vigilant means checking up. When you're used to dealing with Play Doh in the dish water and gum in the hair and ducks in the toilet, a neighborhood barbecue can be a place to gather your wits. A chance to connect with mature friends who will not ask you to answer a hundred questions, tie their shoes, and bring them lemonade.

Ahh…it's so easy to rest the feet and let loose the tongue.

But a social gathering is a place to be vigilant. How can we keep tabs on the small fry and still enjoy the evening?

Here are a few suggestions:

—Work with the other parents. If everybody makes a round to check up, no one is exhausted and everyone has time to chat. Have the understanding that if one of the other parents sees your child misbehaving, they'll alert you right away.

—If the children are playing outside, have the parents sit outside, too. That way you'll be quick to catch discord or improper conduct.

—Have a couple dads or moms play with the children. You can switch off through the evening. The children love this, and you can rest knowing they're under reliable supervision.

—Don't be afraid to make restrictions for after dark. Many, many abuse cases happen when children are left to themselves in the dark.

Being vigilant can be hard. We may need to give up time with our friends or stay away from certain places. Like Gina, we may get bogged down by sunburned dolls and meatballs heading north instead of south. That's when we need to be reminded of our vision. That's when we need a hug from The Knight and a "we're in this together; we'll make it."

2. Preparation. A lot of us think talking to our children is a good idea. But we're slow to get around to it. The days brim and blur. We sew the garments, can the cherries, and swing the hoe. We wash lime Jello off sticky faces, put on Band-Aids, and fetch vases for the dandelions. We bake pie for The Knight and wade with him through poison ivy to look for warblers. Where is the time for clandestine talks on purity?

Maybe we really don't mind not having time. Maybe we think it's too hard to put the rubber to the road. We feel insecure and doubtful. How do you explain abuse to a child without instilling fear?

Maybe you're uncomfortable talking about the facts of life. You stammer and blush and would rather be out in ninety degrees hilling potatoes. You don't know how much is proper to say at what age. Maybe you reason that nobody ever talked to you, and you turned out okay, so your children should too.

What if, because it's hard and uncomfortable, you do nothing, and then your little girl gets picked off when she's out picking daisies? That is ten times harder.

Children have a natural curiosity about the facts of life. Don't stifle it or make them think it's dirty. Channel it.

Telling your three-year-old to keep her dress down is good; what if you take it a step further? Explain how her body is a special treasure, just like the quarters that Grandpas gave her for her birthday. Does she throw the quarters into the toy box or take them along to give milk to the cats? Why not? Some things are so valuable that we must put them in a special place to keep them safe.

Keeping her dress down is part of keeping her body safe. Other people should not see her legs or panties. Those are private.

In a calm, matter-of-fact way, tell your daughter that if anybody ever tries to pull her panties down so they can see or touch her private parts, she should come tell you right away. Assure her that you will not be upset with her, but that you are there to keep her safe.

The majority of abusers seem like nice persons. They can be anybody—friends, relatives, or siblings. They will often set the victim up by taking an interest in them. They'll give them swing rides, help them raid sparrow nests, or whatever it takes to win the child's confidence and trust. Often the transition from friendship to abuse is so subtle that the victim is hardly aware it's happening. The abuser may first invite the child to sit in his lap. Later he may gently stroke her legs while telling her what a good friend she is. Eventually he may explore her most sacred treasure—maybe even rob her of her virginity.

Other times, abuse comes more aggressively. Some victims are chased down and wrestled. Others are grabbed by surprise.

However it happens, it's tragic. As parents, be aware that the majority of children *do not tell their parents what happened*. Many times they've been bribed or threatened to keep silent. Sometimes they're afraid that no one will believe them. Their confusion is so great that they don't know how to express it. They feel a deep sense of shame and are afraid Dad and Mom will say it's their fault and will punish them.

Just as important as preventing abuse is creating an environment that makes it safe for the child to open up if she is abused.

Which brings us to:

3. **Relationship.** Sometimes as I roll the pie crust, I remember the years when I could do it fast and efficiently. Now small hands get mixed up with mine. There is flour on the nose, the feet, and the ceiling. Scraps of dough get turned into a face mask. An eggshell

sails on the spicy surface of pumpkin filling.

I can send her off so I can bake without aging prematurely. Or I can keep her here because this is how she learns. Because quality time is worth more than quality pie.

Having your child confide in you starts long before the abuse. It starts when she helps with the pies, when you dab baking soda on her bee sting, when you add a squirt of caramel sauce to her glass of milk.

It starts when you honor her. When you welcome her presence. When she knows she is more important than the twenty-one things on the to-do list and the friends here for coffee.

She can count on you because you've proven yourself. And when the neighbor boy goes home and shame weighs down the skipping feet, she can come and whisper the words: "Something happened today, Mom."

Your approach to purity should always be calm and on an even keel. Don't dramatize bad men doing terrible stuff to little boys and girls. Don't present facts in an urgent or agitated voice. This plants fear! Your goal is to keep them innocent and carefree, yet have an understanding on certain rules:

—If anybody ever wants to see your privates, or show you theirs, scream for help.

—The person touching you may say it's okay, it doesn't matter, or that he'll hurt you if you tell, but always, always tell anyway.

Don't discuss these rules at age three and expect your child to remember them at four and five. Slip in reminders when you're ready to attend a family gathering, when you drop her off at a babysitter while you shop for paint, when her friends come over for a birthday party. Don't make a big deal out of it, just a little comment here and a question there. You want the rules to be current, but not so overstressed that it causes her to become paranoid.

Make a habit of asking your children questions about their

interaction with other children or adults. This helps them become comfortable with expressing their feelings and may also draw things out they wouldn't tell otherwise.

If your child shares something that raises red flags in your mind, *don't become upset.* Maybe Michael tells Gina that an upper grader at school asked to watch him go to the bathroom. Gina's first impulse is to grab Michael by the shoulder and holler, "What! You didn't do it, did you? Tell me you didn't do it!"

Michael is confused and embarrassed by the boy's request. He is looking to his mother to help him sort it out and reassure him. Instead she gets completely undone. Michael shrugs off her agitated questions and slinks off to the swing under the plum tree. So. When something scary or weird happens, better not be telling Mom!

On the other hand, what if Gina swallows her panic and says calmly, "So, then what? Did you do it?"

This gives Michael a safe premise to share further details. Gina listens and asks questions until she has the whole story. Then she says, "You're a brave little man to tell me this. How about we talk it over with Dad this evening? He'll probably have a good idea what we should do about it. Right now I'm hungry for some brownies and milk. How about you?"

Michael hums as he gets two granite cups and fills them with cold, frothy milk. Break time with Mom!

A close father-daughter relationship is foundational in preventing abuse. It is easy for a dad to feel close to his infant daughter when she splits into a million-dollar smile at the mere sight of him. What about when the daughter grows up and her interests and problems are decidedly feminine? That's when many fathers withdraw. It's easier to let Mom attend the tea party under the kitchen table and smooth out first grade feuds.

Yet a daughter craves her daddy's involvement. Knowing he'll protect her from the neighbor's dog, make her laugh when she's sick, and tell her she's as pretty as her mama will give her a sense of security and contentment.

If the father is passive or absent, or if his involvement doesn't stretch further than correcting bad behavior, the little girl will have a void. She will be susceptible to any man who will make her feel special and beautiful—even if he has evil intentions.

On the other hand, a son who is close to his mother, and whose mother plants in him a high respect for the sanctity of womanhood, will be very unlikely to take advantage of little girls.

Modesty. We all know about that. We all agree it's necessary. But it's touchy because we have different ideas on what constitutes modesty. One family is comfortable with their children walking around the house in their nightclothes. Another family is appalled at the very idea. Gina wears cape dresses for everyday. Her neighbor thinks she's prudish.

So who's to say? If we're honest, a lot of us would admit that at home we don't like to feel dressed up and stuffy. We want space to air out, be comfortable—old, raggy clothes are more comfortable than Sunday clothes, right?—and oh, yes, our heritage! *Make it do. Wear it out.* We justify the too-tight or too-thin dress because back in the Depression, they would've worn it with thanksgiving!

Have you considered that questionable clothes may whet a boy's appetite for the female body and motivate him to explore little girls?

It is a wise mother who takes a special care when she's expecting or breastfeeding. You may think it won't affect you adolescent son to get an occasional glimpse, but many sons have been started on the thorny road of immorality through carelessness of their mother or sisters.

But neither should you wear a refrigerator box just so no one notices you're a woman. Ask God—and your husband—to help you find a balanced perspective.

4. Prayer. Sometimes you do all the right things, you take all the precautions, you have The Talk, and your child still ends up the victim of abuse. This is very painful for parents. It is easy for them to blame themselves and think they should've done something more. You need to realize that you're not God. It is impossible for you to keep an all-seeing eye on your children. We live in a broken world and sometimes we get pierced, no matter how careful we are.

If your child does get abused, by all means do not treat the issue with secrecy. If you feel at a loss how to deal with it yourself, find someone who can help you. Many times when parents cover up abuse, the victim will later become an abuser himself. Doing to someone else what was done to him medicates in a small way his own pain and powerlessness. Deal gently but thoroughly with your child's heart and keep the cycle from being repeated!

The brain power behind Gina's survey was anti-Christian. What do Christian parents desire most for their children? Purity in body, yes, but more, purity in heart...*for they shall see God.*

We want desperately to be good parents, yet we have a way of falling to the far left of our desire—we sit behind the locked bathroom door, angry at the small fists hammering. We turn away from the hurt in our child's eyes because the day has been too full of "trivial" woes. We see the son tickling the daughter in an inappropriate place, but we're just ready to add the spices to the pot of pizza sauce...

What does it take?

A kneeling. If the hands are pinning the diaper or kneading the bread, then the heart can kneel. Crying out for the sons and daughters. Pleading grace. Wrestling for wisdom.

If anything else is effective—the teaching, the talking, the sweating—it begins here. Where stony clods tear our flesh and bloodstained wood rises up. ✻

TRAUMA

Rachel M Stauffer

This is not one person's actual story, but an example of what does happen to some people, how trauma affects the victim, and the role treatment plays in healing. This is only one angle of trauma; it wears many faces. It is not known exactly why one person can work through a terrible happening and then be okay, and the next person finds her life in shambles. Someone like Teresa will need long-term therapy and close support from her community. With this, there is hope for her future.

Teresa was a tiny girl when the stranger did scary things to her. After that she never liked little rooms. She could not tell why. She wanted to be in the big outdoors where there were no walls and only the sky for a roof. There she could run and play in the grass and cuddle her kittens and forget how afraid she was of the dark. When Mom and Daddy sent her to bed every evening, she would lie with big eyes looking into the black, and her heart thumping fast. Only Teddy Bear shared the night with her. Sometimes she had bad dreams and woke up crying. Then she would tiptoe down the stairs and huddle outside her parents' door. Once she ran inside and jumped on their bed, sobbing. She never did it again, for Daddy scolded her and said big girls don't cry, and she should go back to bed, and Mom said she would wake the baby.

School was fun. Teresa liked learning new things. Reading opened a new world to her imagination. But things changed slowly; one day Teresa noticed she was different from the other little girls. She was not sure what it was. She did not fit in, so she started spending time alone in corners of the playground. When the teacher made her join the rest in running games, she stuffed the tears down inside and didn't let anyone see how scared she was. One day a bigger boy tagged her and she fell; she screamed in fright, and laughter bounded around the playground. Teresa determined to never let anybody see her fear again.

The lessons grew harder. Teresa did not sleep well at night and it was difficult to focus on her books. Out of secret habit she popped her thumb in her mouth and sucked on it as she gazed out the window. A snicker plucked her from the reverie and she blushed crimson as the boys smirked. Recess became torture as nicknames pinged on the shell she wrapped around her in hard layers. She would *not* let them see how it hurt.

Worse yet was the time she woke up and her bed was wet. Daddy spanked her for it; he said she should be ashamed of herself. Shame was added to shame. The children were cranky, Mom was hiding in her bedroom after an argument with Daddy, and Teresa had to get breakfast and pack her own lunch. She did not have time to take a shower. Children can be cruel, and the smell brought her new nicknames. Teresa lost all hope that people would ever like her. She became aware that she didn't even like herself.

A new teacher came to school. Teresa kept her distance; no use trying to get this one to like her and be disappointed again. When Teacher tried to peel the shell from Teresa, she hardened it. But one day—she didn't know why—she let down her guard a tiny bit and the feeling of love she got from Teacher was so strange and so full of light! Teresa felt excitement stir—maybe life could hold more times of feeling like this! Then she remembered that she was a bad person and did not deserve happiness. She must not let it happen again. Teacher never was able to get close again.

Uncle Thomas came to live with them for a summer and help

Daddy on the farm. Teresa stayed away from him; she stayed away from everybody when she could and retreated into her dream world. But her uncle noticed how sad she was and where she would go in the woods to be alone. He followed her. At first she was uneasy, but as he talked, she began thinking that Uncle Thomas was rather nice. He said he could make her happy. He laughed when she told him she did not deserve to be happy. And then he showed her what he meant. Afterwards, he told her she must never tell anybody about their secret or it would be ruined, and he would be so upset he would hurt her family. Teresa lay for a long, long time among the leaves. She couldn't cry. She did not feel like Teresa anymore; she did not feel anything except that the world and everything in it was a big black hole and she was falling in.

Grandma came to visit. Teresa shocked herself by gathering the courage to tell Grandma she wished Thomas would leave because he scared her. Grandma looked at her sharply and told her she was being silly and she should not say things like that. So it was not safe to talk to anybody.

That night Teresa felt tight all over and she couldn't breathe. Her thoughts whirled frantically. She suddenly felt afraid of herself, like she might lose control and do something terrible. She curled up in a ball and wished she could stop existing.

Teresa became a numb person. She could not feel anything except anger. She did not know why she was angry. The anger was so big, she was afraid to look at it. She stuffed it carefully inside, out of reach. There were times she wanted desperately to feel something, even pain, to prove she was still alive, still a person. When no one was watching she went to the kitchen and found a knife.

The knife made her real again. At last she had a sensation of being in control of what happened to her. When life was only mocking echoes and emptiness, she could feel alive again when she hurt herself. She deserved the pain.

The addiction didn't make it all better. Instead, she found herself needing more and more self-inflicted pain to control her world. Life became not worth suffering through. When Teresa joined the youth group she found reinforcement that she was a shameful, pitiful creature who did not deserve to live.

○○

After Teresa was discharged from the hospital, she went to a treatment center where she could get help to put her life back together in a safe place. She had endured more trauma in her brief span than most people do in a lifetime. Humans were not to be trusted in her experience and it took gentleness and consistency to get Teresa to open up the least bit. Gradually she learned that this was a safe place where she would not be mocked, and no one laughed when she started to talk. As she relaxed, the need to hurt herself diminished a little; it was worth resisting the urge and distracting herself to hear affirming words from people she was learning to like. Some days it was so terrifying to be vulnerable that she threw up another protective layer and isolated behind it. Persistence from her counselor, doctor, and mentors kept drawing her out. Her doctor was a gentle, discerning man and she sometimes had male therapists leading the groups; slowly she came to think there might be men who would protect her rather than harm her.

As she worked through the program, Teresa learned things she had never known were possible. All the wretched feelings she knew, but could not put into words, were emotions that had names. There were reasons for them. Trauma, abuse, neglect, and rejection; all the things that had happened to her were important, and how they affected her was important. She learned why she was angry and why she felt hopeless. She learned that the trauma was not her fault, and the guilt she felt was a normal effect. She was not alone! The feelings did not go away, but simply understanding them brought relief and made her feel like a person. She was diagnosed with PTSD (post-traumatic stress disorder). Her doctor prescribed medications that helped with her nightmares, lifted her mood, and took the edge off her agitation.

The team worked with her family and helped them understand Teresa's experience and what she needed. When the abuse had to be reported and Teresa lived in terror of her uncle's threat, her counselor helped her through. Bit by bit, Teresa started to think about things she might want to do in life. The day she realized she was looking forward to something was momentous—and scary. Bad things had always followed hopes. This time she had fun, and it gave her another glimpse into what could be possible.

Trust takes a long time to grow and damaged emotions take a long time to heal. Teresa's family was learning, and they agreed with the team that she needed more time in a safe place. She needed time to be a girl; to play games and learn how to interact with other young people. Though the change was hard, Teresa moved to another facility where she would live for a while and continue to learn about trust and life, eventually even to believe that God is good.

Hope is a product of the grace so evident in the lives of people who struggle. ✿

Protecting
THE Innocent
By Someone Who Used to Be

It began in a roomful of four-year-old girls who were curious and silly. I was one of them, with my earliest memory only a whisper, but the picture is a still frame, forever there. We cousins were playing doll and talking about our mean brothers and dolly names and the white kitties in the barn. Then came the daring question, "If you show me your panties, I'll show you mine." We looked at each other to see who would go first. I knew it felt wrong, but in my innocent mind I didn't really know why. But a cousin soon took the dare, and one by one we giggled as we lifted our dresses, then guiltily ran out to play.

Fast forward to another memory of visiting with friends. Once again several of us little girls were playing dolly and decided to make our house in one of the big vans. Inside the van, one girl soon gave the panty suggestion. We giggled as we each took our turn, but then the idea went one step further, and one by one we quickly pulled our panties down then back up.

Childhood innocence. A wonderful God-created gift. But deep in that innocence is the sinful nature that comes with our birth. How quickly this innocence can be ruined and gone. Is it inevitable? A normal part of childhood?

Two years older and again, as friends and I are playing in the bedroom, one of them suggests showing our private parts. We did, but this time it didn't stop with just a quick flash. The play continued for most of the evening until an older sister discovered us and we quickly joined the others outside.

The damage was done. Hidden stirrings had been aroused and awakened. Stirrings that should have lain dormant for years. I didn't understand what I was feeling, but I liked it. It made me feel tickly deep in my belly. When I got a taste of it, I wanted to feel that tickly feeling more and more. And there was something about the secretiveness of it all that made it even more exciting.

I grew up in a very conservative Mennonite home with parents who did well at training us. It was not a dysfunctional home; I felt loved and well provided for. But woven among the biblical teachings, Christian schooling, and modest clothing are these shadowy memories along with the shame of another evening.

A friend was dropped off at our house to stay while her parents went away. We played together until the evening grew long and we became bored. Remembering that secret fun from before, this time I was the one to suggest that we play with each other's private parts and ruined another girl's innocence. My mother happened to open the closed door we thought was locked. After my little friend left, I was taken out to the wood shop and given the hardest spanking of my life.

I wish I could say the story stopped there. And perhaps it would have if a brother hadn't become curious. One night he came into my bedroom, and asked in his six-year-old curiosity to see what I looked like. Then he showed me what he looked like, and once again those God-created feelings that should have been deep in slumber were reawakened. I knew it seemed wrong, and although my brother instigated it, I enjoyed it as well and the feelings it gave me. Under our parents' very noses at times, we'd violate each other's purity with curious looking for the next several years until I was about eleven.

Then came the day my brother became a Christian. He apologized to me for his past behavior and all such conduct immediately stopped. I thank God for His transforming power and forgiveness to each of us. But the memories are not erased.

Through the past years, I've talked with numerous friends, all raised in conservative Christian homes filled with biblical teachings. Were my memories an isolated case? No. Many friends shared their own shadowy memories and secrets, some much more shameful than my own. Who or what failed?

Now a mom myself, I'm determined to not let my children have their own secretive memories. But with my childhood experiences, I tend to mistrust my children and jump to the worst conclusions. A closed door? They're surely up to moral foolishness. Together in a vehicle? No good is happening, and I'm ready to pounce. I imagine the worst before they give me concrete reason to validate my suspicions. I find I'm letting fear parent instead of trust until proven otherwise.

Even though I covet my children's sexual innocence, wanting it to lay dormant, parenting with fear and mistrust is not the answer; I had to lay my fear at Jesus' feet. This is the first step I learned in our parenting journey of protecting the moral purity in my children.

Pray. Pray. Pray. Plead with God for wisdom and discernment in how to guide your children. I pray often for God to protect their innocence, and if something is going on, for us as parents to find out. And already, God answered that prayer in a very unique way, alerting us to something our one child had done. I thank God often.

Communication is one of the next important steps we can take to protect our children. With our swamped schedules, demanding deadlines, and many meetings, we can feel too busy to simply talk with our children about purity and scenarios that can happen.

In looking for advice, I called Life Counseling Ministries and talked with a conservative Christian counselor who helps those dealing with hurting pasts. I asked him, "What would be the main reasons woven through the stories you hear of how or why children's innocence was ruined?"

"Total silence from parents," the counselor said. "It's the number one reason our plain generation is filled with hurting people and ruined lives. Talking about sex and what happens to your growing and changing body was taboo."

Since lips were sealed and because of natural curiosity, children would search out answers—answers that were usually wrong and provocative and led to their ruined purity. Children and teenagers felt they were not free to talk to their parents or ask questions even though they longed to. If something did happen morally, and they would try to talk about it with their parents the answers sometimes were, "It happens to everyone, so get over it."

As parents, we can be tempted to make excuses, thinking our children are too young, or they are good children and would never do such things, or they live in a plain environment that will never expose them to moral compromise. If this is our attitude, then Satan has already broken through the fence. Christian friends, schools, and church are a wonderful blessing, but they don't make us immune to Satan's attacks to ruin our children morally.

Inform your child of what is considered okay or not okay when it comes to their private bodies. Keeping our children in the dark is *not* a gift. Correct information gives them understanding to know when things are right, or if it seems morally wrong and they should be alarmed. If you don't tell them, someone else is eagerly waiting to do the job for you in a way that will ruin the beauty of their God-created sexual being.

How much information is needed and when? The answer can vary from child to child, as children develop understanding and awareness at different ages. But as a girl with memories as young as four and five, we must be proactive at an early age. "Start at three, and give age-appropriate information as they grow," the counselor said.

Bath time is a perfect opportunity to teach our young children basic information. As you wash them, specifically name their different private parts, and mention how no one should ever see it but Mommy. I tell my children, if someone ever asks them to pull down their panties or show their private parts, never, never do it. Quickly run and find me or an older adult they feel safe with. Even if it's one of their own family members who asks, they need to tell me right away.

Don't make it seem as if the child is in the wrong or that they would be the guilty one. Let them know it is a *good* thing to tell. Help children know how to beware when someone says, "Don't you tell. It's a secret." Keep your tone light and matter of fact. Follow up your conversation every so often to let your children know you truly take an interest in their life and to keep repeating the information to engrave it in their mind.

As children grow, so does their need for information about sexuality and the changes that are taking place in their bodies. As we share the facts of life, tell them in a way that shows God's greatness in His design. This is how God created us and how marvelous it is! Correct godly knowledge is one of the best gifts you can give your child.

If your children don't feel comfortable talking with you, they won't be quick to share when a moral violation does take place. Perhaps you have a child that seems uncomfortable talking about sexual subjects, but open the communication line anyway. Talking without eye contact can help make the child feel less uncomfortable. When you're washing dishes, weeding the garden, or driving to town, talk about how babies are born, the pitfalls of pornography, or how to respond to an inappropriate sexual advance. Take your young daughter out for ice cream or on a walk to have an informal but private place to talk. Tell her about her budding breasts and the menstrual cycle and how God is preparing her body for nourishing a baby someday.

Since the world is steeped in sex at every angle, boys especially need to know information and at a younger age than ever before. If their dads don't tell them, they will find out on their own. I know of a ten-year-old boy who knew his mother had some books padlocked in a cupboard. The boy took the cupboard door off the hinges one evening when the parents were gone and read the books.

Again, when sharing with boys, don't make it seem dirty, but let them know they are very normal in their feelings with their bodies reacting in a way God created them. Tell them why they have wet dreams and about the feelings they will experience when seeing scantily dressed women in town. Draw distinct, firm lines as to what is morally right in their responses and what is not.

Tell your older children what words have hidden sexual meanings and are not appropriate to use, such as "queer." They may innocently use them and embarrass themselves, not knowing the world has corrupted the meaning of the word.

Parents are the most important line of protection God has given to children. And according to the counselor's answer to my question, this parental protection is often where the devil breaks through.

"Absence of parents is the second main reason why children lose their purity. They are sent out to play in the barn or playhouse and no adult ever checks on them. At church, children are playing in the basement or classrooms and no concerned parent comes to see what they are doing. You wouldn't believe the stories coming out of church. And when children and teens spend long evenings in their bedrooms without much family togetherness or interaction, these are the situations that have created ideal opportunity for moral purity to be lost."

So check on your children often. Know where and what your children are playing. Yes, it can be a bother when you're deep in conversation or enjoying good laughs with friends. But it is our God-given duty as parents to be responsible. Our children should know Mom or Dad will be checking on them from time to time, and this can keep foolishness from starting.

Create safe boundaries for your child. It isn't a guarantee moral compromise won't happen, but it may help to squash the beginnings. Don't allow play behind closed and locked doors, as seclusion can lead to foolishness and immoral play. This same boundary can apply to playing upstairs or in barns and outside sheds. If children are always wanting to play where no one can see them, it may be a red flag that something could be going on.

Observe your child's play, especially when playing doctor or even mommy and daddy. This type of play seemingly gives children the okay to expose or touch each other, starting them down a road that must remain closed.

Be proactive. If possible, keep girl bedrooms far away or on a different level of the house from the boy bedrooms. This can hinder them from secretly visiting each other's rooms at night. Looking back, this was one downfall of my younger years, as my brother's room was across the hallway from mine.

Be careful with sleepovers. Every parent needs to decide if this practice will or won't be allowed, but use much caution and judgment where you allow your child to sleep-over. Too many children have been violated or exposed to sexual ideas and practices in this environment.

Organize many family times where all children must participate. Whether it's going on a bike ride, reading in the family room, or working in the garden, this togetherness is a way to build communication lines and to keep boredom away. Idleness really is the devil's workshop.

Prepare your child. Even with creating boundaries to protect our children, we can't be everywhere and control every situation. With today's world, we no longer live in an innocent age. It's no longer a matter of *if* our child is exposed to moral situations and pornography, but *when*. "Because of this, the best thing you can do, even overprotecting your child," said the counselor, "is to *prepare them*."

Prepare your sons for the correct response and action needed when they are exposed to pornographic magazines and cell phone pictures or flirty sexual talk from worldly girls. Talk with your daughters and prepare them for a correct response when a man makes lewd comments, a boy exposes himself, or if someone improperly touches them. We teach our children to be polite and respectful and it can be hard for innocent, sheltered girls to know how to be rude to leering men or to scream when they feel threatened.

We can't foresee every situation our children will face in life. But we do teach our daughters how to cook, sew, and garden to prepare them for their own home someday. We teach our sons a trade and how to balance their checkbook and be wise managers in order to prepare them for the day they are leaders in their home. Would we shove them out the door and say, learn the hard way? So why wouldn't we also prepare our children for the bodily changes they will face in life, for the sexual things they'll be tempted with, and for the ways they can protect their purity? Over and above life skills, moral teachings will be one of the biggest blessings we can give our children in the end.

If we as parents band together and stand in the gap for our children with callouses on our knees, then this generation of four-year-old girls will be able to giggle and talk about dollies and the white kitties in the barn, and their innocence will waft to the heavens as a sweet-smelling incense.

I think the angels will smile.

IN MATTERS
GREAT
AND

SMALL
Nora Epp

O ur daughter Lennora was four when she came to me saying
that her cousin Allan had taken her into the cornfield and
removed her panties.

"What else did he do?" I asked. I was sick with worry!

"Nothing," she said. "But why did he do that?"

"Did he touch you?"

"No."

"That was a very good girl to come tell Mother," I said. At the
time, my husband Len and I lived in a single-wide trailer, sharing
our lane with his oldest sister Lisa and her husband Thomas. Len
worked for Thomas and his teenage son in their mini-barn business.

I took Lennora into my lap and talked to her. It wasn't the first
time I had told her to keep her panties on and never let anyone
touch her bottom, but this time I could be more direct with my
instructions—this time she knew that it could happen. "If that ever
happens again," I said, "you holler as loud as you can, and run to

Daddy or Mother. That was so, so good to tell me."

But it wasn't going to happen again, I thought. The very moment that Len came through the door for supper, I told him about it.

"I'm going to call Lisa," I said. "She should know. Or do you want to talk to Thomas?"

Thomas was a quiet man, hard to get close to; I could tell that Len would prefer that I call Lisa. So I did.

"Well," she said, her voice matter-of-fact, "I guess that's what comes of living so close."

"Do they want us to move?" I asked Len later. I felt desperate! Len had wanted us to move for months, perhaps years, and even more so after our twin sons were born when Lennora was three and Rhodes was two. I liked the cozy quarters of our single-wide, the speed with which I could clean the rooms. But was it worth this?

We decided it wasn't. That evening, Len called a real estate agent, and five weeks later, though our twins were only four months old, we were settled into a rancher five miles away on a property of our own.

In the years since, as more children have arrived, with more responsibilities, I remember that incident and wonder whether we did the right thing, or whether we overreacted. I think we made the right choice. (Perhaps the wrong thing was that I waited so long to listen to Len!) I thank God that we could afford to move; we did not have financial complications to take into account.

Thomas never spoke of it to Len, and when I talked to Lisa— once—about it later, she seemed surprised that Allan had not apologized to Len. He had been told to do so, she said. She assured me that they had talked to him. If, truly, nothing else happened, I am grateful for the opportunity it gave us to repeat our instructions to the children.

What happened in the cornfield that day? We may never know. Was Allan curious—but thought better of it before he did anything more? That's what Len suspects. When I had allowed Lennora and Rhodes to play on the swings outside, I thought their cousin was at work in the shop or his mother's garden, back the lane. What if, the next time, Allan would not think better of it? Was it a good idea to keep our children in the house all summer?

I feel confident we did the right thing. But doing the right thing once isn't enough. I am more and more convinced of this. I sit long in my sister's living room with our other sister, and talk and laugh, and mourn the woes of potty-training. The cousins play outside. Len passes the couch on his way to check on the children, and I am smitten—why didn't I remember to do that?

My children are in another room playing and I am in the middle of redesigning a very difficult sewing pattern. For awhile, I hear them singing, "Dare to Be a Daniel." Then they get quiet. Oh, the strength of discipline and love that it takes to go check on them! Sometimes I check on them. But sometimes I don't. I remember that on Thursday when they got very quiet, and I went to check, they were crowded around a small line of ants picking up the leftovers from Tuesday's brownie. Surely they are okay.

Surely—or not?

Let's not hesitate to do a big thing—make a deliberate choice (if it is at all financially feasible) to move away from danger, at home or even in your church community.

But just as importantly, let's not forget to do the little things. Sew bloomers for your daughters. Get up in the middle of an engrossing conversation about potato blight and check on the children. Bathe the boys separately and make it short and sweet. Even though you're tired, or trying to finish canning the last of the green beans, stop by the children's bedrooms a few times until they go to sleep. Listen to their meandering stories so that they will run to you with the tale of what happened in the cornfield.

It's easy to harness the adrenaline to do something heroic. True mother love is a series of small sacrifices performed by an often-weary body for the protection of children whose innocence is priceless, beautiful—and our direct responsibility. 🌼

My Little Child's Plea
Bena Ruth King

Dear mother
please help me today
and be my friend
and be my guide
When I grow up I want to
be just like you
but the road is rough
my feet unsteady
and it feels
so much better when you hold my hand.

Dear mother
when you are not there
so many things
can upset my little world
I want to
be with you now
before I grow up
I want to walk beside you
and it feels
so much better when you hold my hand.

Dear mother
please wait for me
do you have time
to let me help you today
for when you are not around
my world
is upside down
and it feels
so much better when you hold my hand.

Dear Lord
look down on me today
and guide
my faltering footsteps
lest I may stumble
and fall
as I walk through the darkness
of this world
for it feels
so much better when you hold my hand.

Who Are Abusers?
Dispelling the Myths

Brenda Nolt

By having an understanding who sexual abusers are, we will be better able to protect our children from the abuse. There are some widely held false beliefs or myths about abusers. We cannot be effective in protecting our children if we continue to believe these myths, as we may be blinded to the truths or deafened to what victims are trying to tell us. Let us take a look at these myths.

Myth #1. *Most child abusers are "dirty old men" who have serious sexual problems.*

The truth is that while some victims may describe their abusers as such, most abusers are individuals who have families or live in a family setting. They usually have jobs and would never be described as an abuser by those who know them. They will be your father, brother, uncle, cousin, neighbor, teacher, preacher, grandfather, or others. In addition, female abusers cannot be described as "dirty old women." Instead they are normal-looking people known as babysitters, friends, mothers, aunts, grandmothers, sisters, and others.

Myth #2. *Most child abusers do not know their victims.*

The truth is that most abusers select children whom they are related to or know. These children are available to them in ways that other children are not. The child will already trust him or feel a sense of security with him and believe that he would never do something to him or her that was harmful or wrong. The abuser is often in a position of authority over the child, knows that the child is expected to obey him, and takes advantage of this relationship to use the child.

Myth #3. *Most child abusers are so different from normal people that we should be able to recognize them if we knew what to look for.*

The truth is that most child abusers look just like normal people. While most of them can be described as emotionally troubled, you will not be able to predict who may be an abuser just from looking at them.

Myth # 4. *Most child abusers have serious sexual problems that cause them to choose children.*

The truth is that child molesters have problems in three areas of human functioning. Aggression, sexuality, and interpersonal relationships.

Myth# 5. *Most child abusers are mentally ill.*

The truth is that only a very small percentage have been found to be mentally ill.

Myth# 6. *Most child abusers would stop if the child just tried harder to make them stop.*

The truth is that the child is not in the position of power to stop the abuse. Because of the inequality of the child and the abuser, the child never really does give true consent to the abuse. This is true even if the child does not fight off the abuser or ask for help. There are many reasons for the child's compliance and silence. Neither resistance nor struggling is likely to be effective in stopping the abuse from continuing.

Myth# 7. *Most child abusers choose girls, so we do not need to worry so much about our sons.*

The truth is that by far the largest percentage of victims are girls with male abusers, especially if it is occurring within the family. However a very large percentage of child sexual abuse by a stranger or non-family member is directed at boys. There are also cases of abuse within the family where both victim and abuser are males, or both victim and abuser are females. We need to remember that the inequality between adults and children exists for all children—boys as well as girls.

Myth #8. *Most child abusers are males, so we do not need to worry so much about female offenders.*

The truth is that while most child abusers are males, we need to be aware of the safety of our children at all times. Female abusers are more common than most people would think. They will abuse male or female victims.

Myth #9. *Most child abusers are somehow influenced by the appearance or the behavior of the child to commit the sexual abuse.*

The truth is that nothing about the child justifies the choice to abuse him or her. Young children are not seducers even when they act out their abuse in sexually suggestive ways. This is a symptom of what was already done to them, not the cause.

Myth #10. *Most child abusers only abuse one child and then only a few times.*

The truth is that adults that are known to be child molesters say that they committed their first abuse at an average age of 16 and that they have abused many victims. They will continue to do so for an average of three years or until they are found out and stopped. If they are never found out they may look for other children or abuse several different children at any one given time. Reportedly, the average age of the victim in cases of abuse within the family is eleven years of age, with the abuse starting when she is between five and eight.

∘∘∘

We do not know of any social, mental, physical, spiritual, or emotional factors that allow us to identify all or most sexual molesters. Even though many of them are emotionally troubled, so are many other people who never molest children. Even though many of them have had a very troubled childhood or were abused themselves when they were children, so have many other people who have never gone on to molest children themselves. One thing that may help us understand is that many molesters feel that the culture has given them permission to misuse children. These molesters then lack a sense of emotional relatedness—human connectedness—to others. Many of their attitudes and beliefs about aggression, sexuality, and interpersonal relationships come directly from the way boys and men are taught and socialized. Their justifications for the abuse are mirrored in widely held views about women and children.

Denial and blaming the victim are the common responses of child sex abusers. They are also the common responses of most families experiencing incest in their homes or in their churches. Therefore the victim goes unprotected and revictimized and the abuser walks among us unaccountable and unchanged. Communities, churches, and families that stop the denial and victim blaming, provide protection, seek help, and stop the abuser also open the door to healing, recovery, and truly caring as a community. ✿

Protecting Our Daughters

Brenda Nolt

The work of protecting our daughters should be taken seriously. In this day and age when pornography is readily accessible and reportedly one in three girls are abused we should be very concerned about their safety and protection.

One of the best ways we can do this is by teaching them. This is a very important part in their protection. One of the first things we want to teach our little girls is modesty. Tell them to keep their dresses below their knees. Teach them the proper way to sit, with their knees together. They should be taught to give attention to who is across from them and if others can see more than what we would think, especially if they are sitting on the floor or with their legs elevated. This is especially true for homes that have both boys and girls but should also be taught to those that have only girls for when they are away from home. This takes consistency and vigilance on the mother's part.

In the same way, sons should be taught, "Do not look." It does not matter if it is the one-or two-year-old running out of the bathroom undressed, a sudden gust of wind grabbing a dress, or someone falling from the swing. Teach them to quickly avert their eyes and look the other way. This will come in helpful when they are older and they will want to do the same thing for indecent billboards, scantily dressed people in town, or magazines in the stores.

Teach them about proper touching. Tell them that there are parts of their bodies that belong to themselves alone and are not to be seen or touched by anyone else. They are private. This is also very true of children that are playing doctor or pretending they are animals. Make sure they know that if anyone ever tries to do anything like that they should let you know right away. You may want to tell them that if they are sick or hurt that you or the doctor may need to see or touch them and that is okay, but make sure they know how important it is to tell if it is ever anyone else.

Teach them the facts of life. Girls may be able to learn these facts eventually by themselves or in a distorted way from other children, but it is much better if they learn them from their mothers. There are various books available to help you with this subject. If you talk about these things with them it creates a special bond between you. Tell them it is like a special secret from God in how He created us and that it is okay to talk about it with Mother but not anyone else. If you do this with your girls and any type of abuse would happen to them, they will know it is okay to talk to Mother about what happened. This is much better than the spoken or unspoken rule in most homes that we do not talk about such things. This teaching of the facts is also true for fathers and their sons.

Along with teaching our daughters, we also need careful vigilance. Never leave your daughters alone with boys that are older than they are. Yes, even your own sons. We may think that we trust our sons, and we do. It is the devil that we don't trust. He does not care whose life he ruins or how he does it. Know where your daughters are and who they are with at all times. Watch for your daughters' reaction when told that they will be spending time alone with Dad. Do they show fear or reluctance? If they do, you will want to check into it. On the other hand, if they, and you, have a good relationship with their father and you can freely talk about these things with him, there should be nothing wrong with leaving them alone with their father.

What about the time they spend playing with brothers, cousins, friends, or neighbors? You as a mother need to observe, watch, and listen. Is there any sign of inappropriate touch? Do the boys look at the girls in their faces or do their eyes linger on their bodies? Do they have a leering look? Does the girl show signs of extreme anger towards one or more of her brothers, which could be an indication of abuse? This may be true even if they have a special close-knit bond with each other. Mothers often have a special intuition or sixth sense of knowing when something is wrong, so use that God-given gift, and if something does not seem right, look into it further. Do not be afraid to ask questions and make sure that the boys know what appropriate play is.

If you have been abused as a child by your father or an uncle or older brother, don't ever leave your daughters alone with that person and teach them that they are not to sit in his lap. While we do want to come to a place of forgiveness and release to those that have hurt us, we will not forget that the protection of our daughters is more important than any kind of trust we may have built with former abusers. If abuse has happened, we do not forget. In fact, if we want our daughters to come to marriage pure and untainted by the evils of abuse, we do well to never forget or become careless for the sake of our own children's safety.

Another way of protecting our children is to take a walk to all of the bedrooms after they are in bed at night. This will give your daughters a sense of security that if Mother comes to check on me every so often at night she cares that I am safe and okay. Check on your sons too. They will not be tempted to do wrong if they think that this might be the night that Mother will come and see that they are all in their beds. Another thing that we will need to look at is, are our husbands missing from our beds at any time during the night? If they are, please go look where they are. If you are the unfortunate person that finds abuse happening, please do something about it. Go for help. Any amount of shame and disgrace is not worse than letting abuse continue. Be brave. Protect your daughters. Don't let abuse remain hidden. Reveal secrets so they are secrets no more. The damage to our daughters and the future generations is much worse than having abuse uncovered.

All of these things are needed and important for the protection of our children, but there is another, maybe even more important way of protecting our daughters that mothers may be unaware of. That is through relationship. Do you have a relationship with your daughters? Are they your friends? Are their emotional needs being met? Why is it that in some families only one girl is abused? Often it is a child that is more withdrawn and not as vocal about her needs and so they go unmet. This child will then be much more susceptible to abuse, because she will take any type of attention as a means of fulfilling her emotional needs and longings. This is the piece that many people may not understand or be aware of. Not always, but often, the hurting child that is seeking something to fulfill her longings is the one that will get hurt.

Do you really *see* your child? Does she have problems with nervousness, behavior problems, or extreme anger problems? Does she seem withdrawn, preoccupied, absent-minded, or sad? Sometimes children are being neglected, and the painful truth you may not want to look at is that the one who is guilty of the neglecting them is you. Are we willing to go to great lengths to help the child that we struggle having a relationship with and work at

..building that relationship?

So how do we form a relationship with our daughters? The first place to start is with ourselves. Do we have a good relationship with God? Do we spend time in Bible reading and prayer? Ask the Lord to help you have a good relationship with your daughters. If you have been abused as a child and never received help or counseling, go for help now. You cannot fully see your own children's needs until you have come to a place of healing and wholeness yourself.

One of the best ways to fill their needs is to tell them that you love them. Some children need not only to be shown love, but they also need to hear the words spoken to them. How many a hurting adolescent has been lured into a relationship with a boyfriend to fill that deep longing of endearing words of love, only to find that kind of love cheap and unfulfilling? So tell them often how much they mean to you and that you are glad they were born.

Just as important as words of love is touch. Hug them and kiss them and hold them. You can do even simple things like when you are reaching around them, put your hand on their shoulder instead of avoiding touch. Give them good bye, good night, good morning, or get well hugs. While there does come a time when it is inappropriate for mothers to be embracing their sons, or fathers their daughters, it is always okay to give a firm handclasp or a hand on the shoulder. If you have not done this on a regular basis from little on up it may seem awkward and they may even move away from your touch. If this is true for you, begin in small ways and keep it up. Soon you will be able to feel that they are more comfortable with it, especially for those that are craving it. Touch can do wonders to fill the emotional needs of some children. One girl said that immorality was the terrible price she had to pay to be held and thus to mean something to someone. We would think, *mean something to someone*? How could the pain of abuse make someone feel like they mean something to someone? But the pleasure that may be felt in abuse is what that child has been longing for, maybe for a long time. So hold them on your laps as long as they still fit, yes, even after they no longer fit. Fill their needs for touch.

Time is as important as words of love and touch. When your child is speaking to you, look at them and listen to what they are saying. Don't just keep on working and say uh-uh. Look in their faces and make them feel important to you. There may be times that we need to keep at some work or something needs our attention right that minute, but as a rule our children should be more important than our work. Filling the emotional needs of our children and giving them time and attention should always be more important than housework, gardening, or making a living. It is a better gift than food or clothing. In the biblical story of Mary and Martha, it was Mary who chose the good thing. Make them feel wanted and included instead of like they are just in the way. Don't *work* with them. Instead, work *with* them. The emphasis should be on the child, not on the work. Respect their needs, desires, interests, and emotions. The golden rule applies to children as well as adults. How are we really treating them, and how are we, and others in the family, making them feel? Why is it so much easier to be critical and notice what they do wrong, instead of seeing the good in them? Who is the one that is hardest to get along with? Here also, it may not be easy to admit this, but sometimes the one that is hardest to get along with is Mother. Don't give up. Damaged or hurting relationships can be restored.

Keep the channels of communication open between you and your children from when they are little and on up. Ask them where they were, who they were with, what they did, and even what they had to eat. If they know that Mother is always concerned about them, where they are, when they will be back, and what they were doing when they are little, it will not seem so difficult to keep sharing these things when they are teenagers. At the same time, don't make them feel as if you don't trust them. Here again, tell them that you do trust them; it is the devil that you don't trust and he is very busy all the time. Knowing that they are accountable to their parents can help your teenagers resist the temptations that come their way. If you are able to do this you may be able to protect them from the adolescent abuse that sometimes happens to those that were abused as younger children.

The work of protecting our daughters does not need to make us fearful and wary of all the people that our children interact with. But at the same time we will want to maintain an attitude of vigilance and never forget that protecting them is a full-time job. Pray for their guardian angels to watch over them when you cannot be with them and ask continually for God's protecting and guiding hand over their lives. When your daughters reach adulthood, and possibly marriage, pure, clean, and unblemished it will be worth it. May the Lord bless all your efforts.

BECAUSE
I Love Her
Anonymous

"Because I Love Her" is a series of stories illustrating the importance of communication between mother and daughter on the intimate issues of life. Follow Karla and Lisa as they learn from their mothers about the way God has created them. Learn the wisdom of open communication and the consequences of a lack of guidance in these areas. These stories were written with the intent to inform the reader on ways to be open with our children to adequately prepare them for life.

STAGE 1

Karla She bounced in the door to get a drink of water. Playing in the sandbox made one thirsty! Her little playmate—her brother—had gone off with Daddy, and she had soon tired of digging holes by herself.

"Karla," Mom called from the sofa.

Karla twirled into the living room. Mom's nap must be over now.

Sure enough, Mom was stitching at the hem of Karla's new dress.

"Come, sit down," Mom said, patting the sofa beside her.

Something in Mom's voice and the look on her face caught Karla's attention. Mom was excited and very happy about something. She could tell by the tone that Mom had something nice to tell her. "What, Mom?" she asked, a bit breathlessly. The excitement was beginning to flavor her own voice too!

"I have something very special to tell you," Mom began. "God is sending us a miracle. Do you know what a miracle is?"

Karla thought of loaves and fish, and sick people being healed, and she looked questioningly at Mom.

"A miracle is something only God can do," Mom said. "And God is sending one to us. He is sending us..." Mom paused, "a baby!"

Karla gasped and looked at Mom in disbelief. "I was praying for a baby," she exclaimed.

"I know you were," Mom replied. "And now God is answering your prayers! Isn't God wonderful?"

Karla began to giggle. A baby! She giggled and giggled. She bounced off the sofa again and grabbed Mom's hands. "When, Mom?" she asked. "When will we get the baby?"

Mom reached for the calendar lying beside her. Karla hadn't even noticed it. Together they counted the calendar pages. One, two, three, four. They must wait four months until God would send the baby.

"Mom, where is our baby now?" Karla wondered. "Is God making it right now?"

"Yes, He is," Mom said. "Babies are very special and it takes a long time to make them. God has a special place for babies while He's making them. He tucks them inside their mommy until they are big enough to be born."

"Is our baby inside you?" Karla asked in an awed tone.

"Yes, it is," Mom said. "That way it stays safe and warm, and it can grow."

"But how do you know it's there?" Karla wondered. "And how will it get out?"

Mom smiled and hugged her. "God has a special way of telling a mommy that a baby is there," she told her. "And God also has a special way for babies to be born. There is a special little baby door for the baby to come to us when it's big enough, and when you are older, I will tell you all about it."

Karla just couldn't stop smiling. What a wonderful thought! They would have a baby in their own house. Then she thought of something. "Mom, is it a boy or a girl baby?"

"We will wait and see," Mom told her. "You may talk to me or to Daddy about the baby. But it is to be a special surprise for others. For now, it is our secret."

Karla's prayer was worded quite differently that evening. "God, thank you, thank you!" she exclaimed. "I will take good care of the baby You are making for us."

And throughout those one, two, three, and four calendar pages, Karla and Mom shared many happy moments gathering baby clothes and finding a pacifier and sippy cup. Karla dug into the toy box to find baby toys. And she thanked God daily for the new baby He was sending.

ooooooooooooooooooooooooooooooooooooooooooooooooooooooooooooooooooo

Karla turned back to hug Mom as she went out the door with Grandma and little brother Lamar. Excitement bubbled inside her in a way that made her feel like running and shouting. Mom had told her that God had decided their baby was ready to live with them now. God was going to give it to them while she and Lamar stayed at Grandma's!

The next day Karla could finally hold her new baby brother. She gazed at him in pure joy. She examined his hands and caressed his hair. And then she handed him back to Mom and dashed off to her room. "I wanted to tell God thank you again," she explained.

Lisa She bounced in the door to get a drink of water. Playing in the sandbox made one thirsty! Her little playmate—her brother—had gone off with Daddy, and she had soon tired of digging holes by herself.

"Lisa," Mom called from the sofa.

Lisa twirled into the living room. Mom's nap must be over now.

"Lisa, I have a surprise to tell you," Mom said, smiling at her. Something in Mom's voice caught her attention. Mom was excited about something.

"What, Mom?" she asked, a bit breathlessly. The excitement was beginning to flavor her own voice too!

"Grandma is stopping in soon, and she said she would like to take you and Nelson along to her house. She said you can sleep at her house tonight."

Lisa stared at Mom for a bit and then exclaimed, "Going to Grandma's! Goody! Can I sleep with Aunt Bethany?"

"If that's where Grandma tells you to sleep," Mom said. "Now you go get a nightie and a dress to take along."

But Lisa was so excited she barely heard. "Aren't you going along, Mom? Don't you want to sleep at Grandma's?"

Mom smiled. "No, I'm not going along this time. Just you and Nelson are going to Grandma's. Run now and get a nightie. Grandma will soon be here."

The next day Grandma brought Lisa and Nelson back home again to see their new baby brother. Lisa crept into the house quietly as Grandma had instructed her to do. Was it really true? Was there a baby in their house?

It was true! Mom was sitting on the rocker with a blue-wrapped bundle in her arms. Lisa stretched on tiptoes and leaned forward to look. "Can I hold him, Mom?" she whispered.

Mom smiled. "Sit down here on the sofa and I'll put him in your arms."

Lisa cradled her tiny little brother. He scrunched up his face and squirmed. She gave him a gentle kiss. "Oh, Mom, he's so cute," she exclaimed.

Grandma chuckled and reached out for her turn. Lisa let her take him, and then she began to look around. In the corner was a tiny baby bed that hadn't been there yesterday. She ran over to check it out. It was lined with such soft blankets. A burp diaper was draped over the edge. And her wondering mind formulated an answer to the unspoken question. The baby had been in this bed, but where had the bed come from?

She asked her mom later where the bed had come from, and Mom looked surprised. "From the attic. Don't you remember when Nelson slept in that bed?"

Lisa didn't remember, but now things did not make sense again. She knew the baby hadn't come from the attic. "But Mom, I thought you got the baby in that bed. Where did the baby come from?"

"God sent the baby," Mom replied in a tone that implied the conversation was over. "Here, please go fill my cup with water."

Lisa did. But she didn't stop wondering. Somehow, though, she knew she shouldn't ask Mom again. She knelt to say her prayers that evening, and she thanked God for the baby. But her little heart expressed no joy to the Giver of the baby, only a shade of reproof for sneaking the baby to their house while she was away. Then she crawled into bed to wonder some more. Had God dropped the baby down from Heaven? If she went to Grandma's house again, would He send another one?

Congratulations! God is sending you a baby!

The joy of that reverberates through a mother in a way that is truly indescribable. After realizing that truth, a change takes place within the deepest part of a mother that changes the way she eats, sleeps, thinks, and plans her schedule. Her prayer life changes, her emotional awareness is acute, and she focuses on the next nine months in a way she wouldn't have before.

Whether she is feeling overwhelmed by the news, or whether extremely excited, a woman has a constant awareness of the new life growing inside her from the moment she realizes that she truly is expecting a baby.

In the next months, she will alter her life because of that new little being, and also prepare in many ways for her life to change again when the baby arrives. Her husband may not always understand the constant awareness and changes, and she may not always understand herself, but the absolute truth is that from the moment she knows that life is growing within her, she is totally in tune with it.

That is why a miscarriage or a stillborn baby is so very painful to go through. The baby is truly "her baby" the minute she knows of its little existence.

For a mother with other children to care for it may at times be difficult for the rest of the family to "understand" Mother during those nine months. Some parents choose to hide the fact that a baby is on the way. They go to great lengths to make sure none of the children figure it out.

Be that as it may, there are other ways to deal with the fact that a baby is on the way that is totally proper and not being indiscreet. It can be such a blessed time of anticipation, not only for the family but for the other siblings as well. It also creates a feeling of kinship within your own family that can open great doors later in life in the areas of communication.

My husband and I chose to tell our children around the sixth month of my pregnancy. That time of sharing was so very special. We didn't give many details, very like Karla's mother, but were open and honest with their questions. If they persisted with questions we were not comfortable answering for their age, we told them the same thing Karla's mother did, "We will explain more when you are older and better able to understand. It is too hard for you to understand right now." Just as you are careful to give your child age-appropriate chores, so you must be careful to present them with age-appropriate information.

Often we would tell them that God has an amazing way of taking care of everything and we don't have to worry about it. I remember my oldest son saying, "So it's really a miracle?" And without a doubt, we could tell him, "Yes, it truly is a miracle from God."

Children are so accepting of what they are told. If you are matter of fact and open, not showing shame or rebuke, they will not see it as anything other than what you say. The miracle of new life strengthens their faith in a way I was amazed to watch. My daughters dreamed with me as we sorted baby clothes as the day drew nearer. The boys anticipated the arrival of a "brother," of course. Every night, their little prayers wrapped around me and the life growing inside of me. I felt more prayed for with my last baby than with any of the others.

We also were sure to warn the children that the baby has not yet arrived and we do not always know what God's plans are for a new baby. We told them that sometimes God calls babies home before they even get to breathe in this world. And sometimes God allows disabilities. I was astounded at their soberness and their ability to grasp what this would mean. We talked of some families who had to give their babies back to God, and in that way, I felt we got a chance to probe the topic of death in a way they could understand.

All in all, telling my children of the fact that a baby was on the way was very special to all of us. We made it clear that they were not to talk about it with others unless an adult asked them. It was special to have a family secret. During those months of waiting it seemed the secret bound us together in a special way.

But more special was the day the baby finally arrived! The joy on the children's faces was only a mirror of this mother's joy!

A tiny bundle to love and hold—greeted with many hugs, kisses, and admiring touches from the whole family!

It truly is a miracle!

STAGE 2

Karla Karla sat at the table, delight imprinted on her features, fingering, sorting, and studying each treasured item as she arranged it in her pencil box. She rearranged them. Then dumped them out to start all over. She was a first-grader-to-be!

She didn't see Mom smiling tenderly and thoughtfully at her. But she looked up when Mom pulled out a chair to sit beside her.

"I can hardly believe my little girl is going to school," Mom said.

"Mom," Karla exclaimed. "You forgot again. I'm not little anymore!"

"You are right," Mom said. "You are growing up so fast." She paused a bit. "But I wonder if you are grown up enough."

"For what?" Karla wondered.

"You are old enough to go to school and learn to read and write. But are you grown up enough to do what you know you should do even if someone else does wrong?"

Karla nodded emphatically. She was sure she was grown up enough for that!

"Sometimes children might say things they shouldn't say, or treat someone unkindly, or disobey the teacher. And I won't be with you at school. Can you remember to do what you know you should do even when you are away from Daddy and me?"

Karla nodded. There was a sober look in her eyes.

"And there's another thing I want to tell you," Mom said. "Do you remember what Daddy told you to do if someone asks you to come into their vehicle so they can give you a piece of candy or something like that?"

"I should run away and tell you," Karla answered.

"Yes, that's right. Always come and tell us if something like that happens. And if someone ever tells you something bad, or does something bad to you, you must also tell us that right away. Even if they say you must not tell anyone, you must still tell Daddy and me."

Karla looked thoughtful. "You mean like if someone pushes me at recess?"

"It is unkind to push others, but that's not really what I meant," Mom replied. "Sometimes big people touch children in bad ways. If someone that you don't really know ever wants to hug you, you come and tell me or Daddy right away. And if someone tries to touch under your clothes, you say 'No' to them, and come tell us. Then we can help keep you safe."

Karla pondered a moment. "But what if I'm at school, or what if you are busy?"

"If you are at school, you can tell the teacher. Or just tell me as soon as you can," Mom replied. "You may tell me about anything that worries you. We love you and we want to take care of you."

The worry lines slipped off Karla's forehead as she and Mom arranged the precious school articles in the pencil box yet another time. She was free again to look forward to school—with a more complete anticipation than before. Mom had given her a solution to any problem she might face. She could just tell her parents!

"Mom, is it soon time for a school meeting?" Karla wondered. A year and a half had passed since she had innocently dashed into the classroom—into a new grown-up world. She was nearing the end of second grade now.

Mom paused in her supper preparations to glance toward the calendar. "I think it's next week," she said. "Why do you wonder?"

Karla didn't answer right away. Then she said quietly, "I don't want to go to Eli and Nancy's again."

Mom paused for the second time and looked at Karla. "Why not?" she asked, and Karla felt rather than heard the concern in her voice.

"I don't like Curtis," she whispered.

"Tell me why," Mom said as she rinsed her hands and sat down close to where Karla had been folding socks.

"He does things I don't like…" Karla's voice trailed away.

"What does he do?" Mom said in a tone of voice that encouraged Karla to go on.

"Lisa was there too when we stayed there. We played church with the dolls and he was reading in the room where we had church. There weren't enough chairs and he said I should sit beside him on the couch. And then he leaned over and said he wants to see my doll…" Karla stopped again for a bit, and Mom patiently waited.

"And he put his hand here on my leg," she finished, motioning to her upper leg.

"What did you do?" Mom wondered.

"I went out, and Lisa came too, and we stopped playing church."

"What did you play then?" Mom asked.

"We played Uncle Wiggily at the kitchen table. And Curtis came for a drink of water, and he said he wants to watch our game, and he said he would sit on Lisa's chair and she could sit on his lap because there weren't enough chairs."

"Did Lisa do that?" Mom asked.

"No, she just stood," Karla replied. "And Curtis kept saying she could sit on his lap instead, but she didn't."

"Where were Eli and Nancy?" Mom wondered.

"Eli was in his office and Nancy was reading. I was so glad when we could go home," Karla finished.

Mom laid her hand on Karla's arm. "Thank you for telling me," she said in a gentle tone. "That was the right thing to do. It was also good that you got up and went out of the room when Curtis put his hand on your leg. I will talk to Daddy about it, and you will not have to stay there again."

Karla sighed, as if she had unloaded an immense burden. She had. She felt secure and safe and cherished. She was. She felt a deep relief, and all was right with her eight-year-old world again.

Lisa Lisa sat at the table folding washcloths. There was no merry tune on her lips or in her heart. There was a mass of fear instead, that she couldn't quite define. She didn't know what to do about it.

It had begun choking her when the teacher reminded them to clean out their desks for the parent-teacher meeting. She had organized her desk just like the rest were doing, and no one realized the lump of dread she suddenly harbored. Now it was all she could think about.

She wondered where Mom had made arrangements for them to stay, but she was afraid to ask. She knew she did not want to go to Eli and Nancy's house again. But how could she tell Mom why? Mom would just tell her to ignore Curtis. After all, he really hadn't hurt her.

But deep down she knew something was wrong. She knew instinctively that a big boy shouldn't act like Curtis acted, but she didn't really know why. Suddenly she couldn't wait any longer.

"Mom, where are we going to stay when you go to the school meeting?" she asked.

Mom paused in her supper preparations. "School meeting? Oh my, I forgot about it. Well, I suppose you will stay with Eli's again."

"Mom," Lisa said, almost desperately. "Couldn't we go somewhere else? Karla said they aren't going to stay there this time."

Mom sighed. "Well, probably not. Nancy said she can babysit for the school meetings, and besides, they are right along the way to school."

Lisa did not reply and Mom asked, "Why don't you want to go there? Because they have no little children?"

Lisa felt a surge of hope. Maybe she could change Mom's mind. "Curtis…" she paused, "isn't nice to us."

"Well, I suppose he's just not used to children since he's the youngest in the family," Mom said. "I think you can stay there again. You just be kind to him and I'm sure he'll be kind to you. Finish folding those washcloths now, and get the table set for supper."

Lisa turned back to the dwindling pile of laundry, and her heart seemed to flutter. She frantically searched for a solution, and then she thought of one. She would stay in the room where Nancy was until Mom and Dad came back. She would use the bathroom before they left, then she wouldn't need to leave the room for that. She could do without a drink. Then Curtis would surely let her go.

⸺⸺⸺⸺⸺⸺⸺⸺⸺⸺⸺⸺⸺⸺⸺⸺⸺⸺⸺⸺

Do we really have to go there?

Yes, we really do.

It is so much easier to not even think about these things, and yet realistically if our desire is to be a godly mother, we must. The well-being and even the souls of our dear little ones are at stake. It is imperative that we recognize that fact so we can better face these difficult situations head on.

Statistics would say that in the world around us one in three children are sexually abused by the time they are teenagers. As sad and disturbing as that is, it is also determined that 95% of children are exposed to pornography in some form by the time they are teenagers. To hit even closer home, it is stated that in conservative circles the ratio of sexually abused children is one out of seven.

Seriously? Those statistics cause bile to rise in my throat. And if we stay focused there we may become terribly discouraged and depressed.

How can I, as a mother, protect my children from molestation or sexual abuse and misuse?

I don't think we can ever be positively sure that our children will not be exposed or misused. We live in a fallen world, and as time continues, things grow worse and worse, just like the Bible prophesies it will. "Men (and women) become lovers of themselves more than lovers of God..."

Karla's relationship with her mother was open enough that she was able to express to her mother what happened when she was being babysat by the neighbors. Her mother listened to her, and most importantly, didn't shame her, but put her fears at ease by promising to talk to Daddy and take care of it.

Suddenly the burden slipped off Karla's back and onto the backs of her parents who were more able to handle the situation than she was. That is a big part of us protecting our little ones. Children are not able to carry the burden of abuse or inappropriate situations alone. If they cannot express it to their parents, the ones who are put in place to protect them, where can they go with it? Often they will internalize it to the point where it becomes debilitating. It may not happen immediately, but will come out some way. Behaviors change. They become withdrawn and fearful. Or just the opposite—brass and extreme. Sadly, many will lose so much self-esteem that they will determine they are not worthy of love, even God's love, the very One who created them and loves them unconditionally. How sad that must make the heart of our dear Father.

It is of utmost importance that we make even our smaller children aware of protecting themselves in the event that someone tries to take advantage of them. If they are made aware, they will recall your advice and know where to turn.

Again, there is no need to be explicit. A simple description such as; "Sometimes there are children or even adults who may do things to you that you do not like. They may touch you in ways you do not like or that make you feel sad or sick." At this point I will tell them that any time someone touches them underneath their clothes or tickles them in places that they think are not right, they should tell Daddy or Mommy.

Children do not have the concept of sexual advances. In their innocence, they will go along with something most times unless they are warned in advance. If they have an awareness to a certain extent, they will know where to go if they are confronted with something in this line. A simple explanation of what is considered inappropriate will give them enough of an understanding that they will feel more comfortable telling you about it.

Even so, many times they will not talk about it. You will notice that Karla did not tell her mother about Curtis until she realized she might be faced with the situation again. Thankfully, at that time she was able to express herself, and her mother, wisely, did not overreact but assured Karla that it would be taken care of and that she didn't need to worry about it any longer.

As mothers, we may tend to overreact when our children talk to us about these things. Our minds are not innocent anymore and we can immediately see the "evil" in these actions. *But we must be so careful.* If we overreact and scold or grow angry, our children will interpret that to mean they are the cause of our anger. Rest assured, they will not come to us so quickly again. Although we know what is behind these things, we must remember our children do not. Let's not further destroy their innocence by overreacting when we are forced to face the fact that our children may have been involved in something inappropriate.

They need to feel safe, knowing that Mommy will love them no matter what they have done or what was done to them. They need to know beyond a shadow of a doubt that Mommy will take care of it. A very good response would be a gentle hug, and to immediately thank them for telling you. You may need to question them more carefully on what actually happened but be careful not to attack them with questions.

Lisa was not so comfortable with her mother. We need to be careful to really listen to our children. To hear what may be between the lines, because sometimes they are too fearful to come out and say it in words. Or maybe they don't even know how to express their feelings.

If a child expresses reservations where there normally were none, we need to push a little to see why they are feeling that way. Lisa's mother did ask, but when Lisa mentioned that Curtis wasn't nice to them, she didn't pursue it any further. A simple, "What does he do that you don't like?" may have given Lisa enough courage to express herself.

There is a fine line here, because we do not always want to be thinking the worst about a situation either. We need to pray earnestly for wisdom and trust that God will open our eyes to the times when something just isn't right.

Some may call it a mother's intuition; I call it God. Let Him lead you, and if a situation seems puzzling or sinister to you share it with your husband, or if that is not an option, an older sister or brother in Christ. Do not allow shame or fear of what others may think to keep you from protecting your children. Remember their souls may be at stake.

Pray for wisdom, and as promised in James 1:5: *If any of you lack wisdom, let him ask of God, that giveth to all men liberally, and upbraideth not; and it shall be given him.*

STAGE 3

Karla hummed a nameless little tune as she took piece after piece of laundry from the line. Then turning, she dropped each piece into its own wash basket. She and Mom had developed this method of sorting the wash as they took it from the line. Then Mom would fold her and Dad's basketful, Karla would fold her own laundry and Krista's baby items, and one of them would do the three boys' basketful.

Lamar was with Dad. The younger boys were industriously farming in the sandbox out under the tree, and Krista was still napping. Mom was beside her at the picnic table folding clothes. Karla liked these times when she could have Mom all to herself. They could talk about new dresses and program poems, and discuss options for end-of-term gifts for the girls in her room.

Karla unpinned the long line of underclothes. As she dropped a bra into the basket she remembered. "Mom," she said, "Nancy said she wears one of these now."

"I see," Mom replied thoughtfully. "Isn't she in seventh grade?"

Karla nodded. "Is that when I will wear one too?"

Karla didn't hear the prayer in Mom's heart, but she saw her close her eyes just a bit. Then Mom smiled at her, "Time will tell," she said.

Karla looked uncertain and turned back to the wash line. But then Mom went on, "This would be a good chance for us to talk about something special, Karla. You will soon be twelve. You are maturing. I know that because you are becoming more and more dependable. Your body is going to mature too, and I want to tell you about that."

Mom walked over to the screen door to listen if Krista was awake. She wasn't. "Sit down," Mom invited Karla, patting the bench beside her. "We can fold wash while we talk."

Karla slowly pulled a piece from her wash basket. She knew by Mom's actions that she had something important to tell her. It made her feel good—grown-up somehow—to have Mom talk to her like this.

"In the next few years," Mom started, "your body is going to change. Your breasts will grow, and you will start to wear a bra. I'll tell you when it's time to wear one. And sometime you will start to have monthly cycles. We usually call them periods."

Karla still held the first piece of clothing she had pulled out of her basket. She was concentrating on each word Mom said. Mom went on, "When a girl or woman has a period, she bleeds. There is an opening between your legs that will bleed. It's all part of God's plan so that someday girls can be mothers. It bleeds for about five days, and then it stops again. Then in a month it bleeds again for five days."

Karla's hands had totally stopped now. "Does it hurt?" she asked in a near-whisper.

"The bleeding itself does not hurt. Sometimes girls have backache while they are having a period. We call it cramps. And if that happens, taking something like Tylenol helps. But most people do not mind it. There are special pads to fasten to your panties that will absorb the blood. I have some for you, and whenever you see a bit of blood, tell me right away and I will show you how to use them."

Karla didn't say anything for a bit as she processed the

information. Suddenly things made sense. She had somehow known that there was something—a woman thing of some sort—because she'd heard her older cousin ask someone if it was "that time of the month." And then they had laughed about it. She had noticed that the one eighth grader at school didn't always help play at recess without an apparent reason.

Mom calmly went on folding wash beside her. "Will it soon happen to me?" Karla asked.

Mom smiled tenderly at her. "I wish I could tell you that," she said. "But I do not know. Some girls get them at your age, but I think for most girls it starts when they are twelve or older. I was thirteen when my periods started."

Karla looked at her mother. Somehow knowing that Mom had them too made it seem less scary.

"And Karla," Mom went on. "Sometimes girls feel grouchy and cross when they are having a period. Sometimes they feel like crying over something that normally wouldn't make them cry. That is caused by something in your body called hormones, and it is perfectly normal. Tell me if you feel that way."

Karla said nothing, and Mom smiled at her again. "It is a lot to take in at one time, but it is okay. Just tell me as soon as you see some blood when you go to the bathroom and I will show you what to do about it. Most times when it first starts there is only a tiny bit of blood. If you wonder about anything, just ask me. I want to hear your questions."

"Okay," Karla said. And she looked into Mom's eyes and smiled in a way she had never done before. It was a woman to woman smile. She felt as though she had grown up several decades just in the last minutes. She felt like a young woman rather than a little girl, and it felt good. It all sounded a bit scary, but with Mom at her side, and in her confidence, she was almost eager to face it.

Krista began to fuss and Mom stood up. "One more thing, Karla.

This is not something to joke about or discuss with others. You may talk to me about it anytime you need to, but don't talk to the girls at school. Nancy should not have been talking about wearing a bra. It is not a bad thing, but it is not something we talk to others about. It is better to share these things with your mother than other girls."

That evening as Karla lay in bed pondering all Mom had said, she thought of something. The sleepiness vanished from her eyes and her heart pounded at the thought. "What if a period starts when I'm at school?"

She slipped from her bed and went downstairs to where Mom was rocking Krista. She whispered so as not to disturb the baby and Mom whispered back that she would come talk to her when Krista was in bed. She soon came.

"If it happens at school or anywhere that you can't talk to me right away, just get a long piece of toilet paper and fold it until it's the width of your panties. Then tuck it between your legs and pull up your panties over it. Tell me as soon as you can."

Karla relaxed. Mom made it sound as if it were nothing to worry about. "Pray about it," Mom said. "God made you to have periods and He doesn't want you to have to worry about it" Mom sat on the edge of Karla's bed and turned on her little bedside light. She reached for the Bible on Karla's nightstand. "I want to show you some verses."

She turned to Genesis 1, verse 27, and read, "So God created man in his own image, in the image of God created he him; male and female created he them." Then her finger slid down to verse 31 and she read again, "And God saw everything that he had made, and behold, it was very good."

She smiled at Karla. "God made women. He made them to have periods, and then He said it is very good. Don't ever doubt that, Karla. The way God made you is good. It is not something to be ashamed of or scared of. I'm thinking of another verse…"

Mom turned to Psalms and paged around a bit. "Here it is," she said. "In Psalm 139:14. 'I will praise thee; for I am fearfully and wonderfully made.'" She closed the Bible and laid it back. "And fearfully in that verse means amazingly. So the way you are made is amazing and wonderful."

Mom patted Karla's shoulder and stood up again. "Can you sleep now?"

"Yes," Karla murmured. "Good night, Mom."

And slowly her whirling mind relaxed and she drifted peacefully to sleep.

∞∞

Karla gasped. Was it? With a hand that was suddenly trembling, she wiped again. Yes, it was.

Breathlessly, she raced down the steps. Mom was stirring up baked oatmeal, their usual Sunday morning breakfast. "Good morning, Karla," Mom said, then stopped as she noticed Karla's pale face.

Karla glanced around the kitchen. No one else was there, but she could hear one of the boys showering in the bathroom. Stepping close to Mom, she whispered, "There was blood..."

Mom nodded and whispered back, "Go up to your room. I'll be right up."

Karla raced back up the steps as she heard Mom slide the pan of oatmeal in the oven. She sat down on the bed and waited nervously. Mom went into her own room and then tapped on Karla's door.

Karla watched every move as Mom showed her how to fasten the pad to a pair of panties. It seemed crinkly. "Is it—does it—" Karla hesitated. "Can other people hear it crinkle?"

"No," Mom assured her. "It won't crinkle when you are wearing it. Go slip these panties on now and see how it feels. I'll wait here."

Karla went to the bathroom and put them on. "I guess it's okay," she told Mom.

"You'll be fine," Mom said. "It probably won't bleed very much since this is the first time."

But Karla was still worried. "What about church?" she asked.

"It's okay to go out to the bathroom if you feel like you need to check it," Mom said. "But I think it will be fine until after church. We're going to Grandpa's for dinner, you know, and I'll put an extra pad in my diaper bag for you to change. I'll have to go upstairs to change the little boys out of their church clothes. Come along upstairs and I'll give you the pad then."

"Okay," Karla said, in a voice that still nearly wanted to tremble. But she felt better inside.

As Karla followed the girls her age outside after church, she glanced at Mom. Mom was looking at her and Karla could see the questions in her eyes. She smiled, a tiny little smile. Mom smiled back, a reassuring gentle smile.

∞∞∞

"I think it's over now," Karla said quietly to Mom as they worked together on supper preparations four days later. "There was no blood on the pad since this morning."

"Good," Mom replied. "You handled it real well. It probably is over, but wear a pad until tomorrow morning just to be sure. And on the calendar in your room count twenty-eight days from Sunday, the day it started. That is when it will probably start again. It may not be exact, but it will probably be around then."

Karla nodded, but a sigh escaped at the same time. "I'm glad it's done," she said. "It's kind of…scary."

Mom nodded sympathetically. "I know how you feel. It will get less scary with time. Just remember, this is the way God planned for women to be, and it's a good thing."

Women. Karla rolled the word around in her mind long after the conversation ended. She was no longer just a little girl. She was beginning to be a woman. She felt as though she were stepping through the doorway into a huge new world. It looked somewhat frightening, with unknown dark corners here and there. But Mom had done it. Mom was there to help her through the doorway. And although she could not have put it into words, a deep admiration and respect for her mother urged her forward.

Lisa   Lisa gasped and stared. Blood! She grabbed a fresh handful of toilet paper and wiped again. More blood! Her heart pounded and the hand holding the bloody toilet paper felt clammy cold.

Lisa bent over and tried to look where the blood was coming from. She couldn't see anything, and nothing was hurting. But—she wiped again—there was still more blood.

Sweat broke out on her forehead, even though it was rather cool in the bathroom. Lisa tried to think, but nothing made sense. What was wrong with her? How could she be bleeding when nothing was hurting? Something must be seriously wrong—was she dying?

She was trembling now. What should she do? This was last recess, but there was another hour of school yet. Should she tell the teacher that she was bleeding? But how could she go to the teacher? What if the blood ran out on her clothes?

She wiped again and there was only a faint smear. Good, maybe it was stopping now. She stood up. Her legs felt weak and she leaned against the wall. She pressed her hands hard together to make them stop trembling. The other students were coming in now, and she knew she must go to her seat or everyone would wonder what was wrong. Surely it couldn't be anything too bad if nothing was hurting.

Surely she wouldn't die from a little bit of blood.

Seventh grade's assignment for the last class was a spelling workbook lesson, and Lisa filled in answers at a feverish pace. She tried not to think about what might be wrong with her, but it was no use. Then a harsh memory broke into her mind, and she nearly gasped. It must be! That was probably what was wrong with her! And she felt a slight bit of relief. Then at least she wouldn't die right now.

A girl her own age had died of cancer two years ago. It must be cancer that she had! Well, at least she would survive through the rest of the school day.

"Lisa, you look sick," her brother remarked as they walked in the lane.

"Mind your own business," Lisa snapped. She felt sick, but she wasn't going to give him the satisfaction of admitting it.

"Ho, ho," he hooted. "Look out for Lisa! She's in one of her bad moods again."

Lisa blinked back tears and kept her eyes on the lane. She was used to this—trying to hide tears that were threatening to come. She had wondered, at times, why she felt so miserable and grouchy. It must all be part of the cancer.

Mom was not in the kitchen and Lisa ran right upstairs to the bathroom. There was more blood again, and a smear on her panties. She heard Mom over in her room putting wash away, and she heard the boys come upstairs to change. Mom told them to get an apple for a snack and to go out to Dad. They pounded back downstairs.

Lisa still sat on the commode. She didn't know what to do. Somehow she had to let Mom know that something was wrong with her, but how? Then Mom knocked on the door.

"Lisa, are you soon done in there? I want to put some laundry away."

"Coming," Lisa said, and her voice trembled enough that Mom

heard it.

"What's wrong?" Mom asked.

Lisa choked back a sob, but the next one escaped.

"Lisa, are you okay?" Mom asked.

Lisa opened the door. "Something's wrong," she whispered. "I'm—I'm bleeding. I think I have cancer or something."

Mom gasped. "Bleeding! Where?"

"When I go to the bathroom…" Lisa replied, wiping the tears that kept escaping her puffy eyes.

"Oh!" Mom exclaimed. "Did it just start?"

"Yes," Lisa said. "In school. At last recess."

"Well, that's nothing to worry about," Mom said. "That's normal. Wait here a bit." And she hurried to her room.

Lisa stared after her. Normal? This bleeding was normal? Before she could make sense of anything, Mom returned with a pad.

"Here, fasten this to your panties to soak up the blood. You are having a period. It's normal. All women have them. Come down when you are done. I want your help."

Mom headed down the steps, apparently forgetting the laundry she had planned to put away. Lisa mechanically locked the door, then sopped up another flood of tears. Tears of relief. So it wasn't cancer! Nothing was wrong after all!

She unfolded the pad and studied it. So this was normal? All women had bleeding like this? But why? Suddenly growing up looked overwhelming.

Lisa moved woodenly around the kitchen. She felt lost in her own home. She shoved some supper down her gravelly throat. Everyone else acted so happy it irritated her. The tears were just below the surface, and as soon as the dishes were done, she escaped upstairs. She went to the bathroom. Yes, she was still bleeding. How long would this last? At least tomorrow was Saturday and she would not have to go to school.

Mom knocked on Lisa's bedroom door and entered with a pack of pads in her hand. She set them on the cupboard. "You can keep those," she said. "Put a new one on whenever you need it. You'll stop bleeding in about five days." She turned to go.

"Okay," Lisa mumbled, trying to keep the shock out of her voice. Five days! She would bleed for five days! She sat in numb dread. How was she to endure this for five days?

∞∞∞

Lisa sat stiffly on the bench. She didn't even try to concentrate on the minister. This was the third day, and she was still bleeding. She had worried about coming to church until late the night before, now here she was. Was the pad on right? What if some leaked out? Everyone would see it when she stood up to go out. She would have to stay sitting until church was over, then she would rush to the bathroom. Besides, Mom didn't like if she went to the bathroom during church. She wasn't to do that unless it was an emergency.

By the time they were ready to pray, Lisa nearly had herself worked into a frenzy. She could see in her mind the spot of blood on her dress. She could almost feel a trickle on her leg. She hesitated just a bit longer than the rest to kneel down, and then she crouched on spring-loaded knees and listened for the "amen." She was the first one sitting down again.

They began to sing and Lisa noticed a younger girl in front of her singing heartily. "Just you wait," Lisa told her silently and severely. "You don't know what's coming. Be happy while you can." The girl looked so carefree that it brought a lump to Lisa's throat. If only she could be seven again and have nothing to worry about. At least nothing like this!

Lisa glanced at Karla farther down on the bench. Did Karla get these yet? And then she remembered seeing Karla slip something from her coat pocket on her way to the restroom. She had wondered briefly at the time, but now she suspected she knew what it was. Probably Karla had had a period too.

But then again, maybe she hadn't. She looked happy too. Lisa couldn't imagine ever really being happy again. Not with this ominous thing called "periods" lurking near. It was smothering her; it was snuffing out all the fun in life; it was shredding any bits of anticipation for a future of womanhood. She felt shameful and dirty. If only she could go far away from anyone and have this awful period without the risk of anyone finding out. If only she could just stay little and carefree. If only—if only there just wouldn't be any Lisa.

The ever-present tears nearly spilled. Lisa blew her nose fiercely. They were done singing now. She pasted her smile back in place. No one would know how she felt. Maybe if others didn't know everything about her, they would still like her. It was all she had to hope for.

∞∞∞

Your little girl is growing up!

It is an exciting and scary time in a girl's life (as you well remember) when her body starts to change. Though subtle, puberty makes itself known as a gradual "bigger than life" force in the mind of a young girl. She needs her mother during this process to be a stable understanding center in her life.

Who better to understand a young girl's turmoil during this hormonal time than a mother who was once there herself? We mothers need to dig deep into our compassion and remember.

Remember the upside-down cycle of emotions? Remember the feelings when we first started to develop? Remember the scary feeling of facing the first cycle of a lifetime of menstrual cycles?

Remember flip-flopping from total happiness to total sadness in the space of ten minutes? Or even ten seconds? Remember the confusion? The tears? The fears?

Yes, we surely do remember. What greater comfort can be given to a young girl than to know that Mother understands. What a relief to have confidence that Mother will help her through this new phase of life because she was once a young girl herself.

There is a special closeness that can develop between a young girl and her mother when communication is open enough for her to be able to ask questions and not be shamed into silence. Like Karla, your daughter will be much more confident within herself if she has a small understanding of what her body is going through and that it is all okay. For her to understand that it is all part of God's wonderful plan for her to become a woman will help her face it in a healthy manner.

On the other side, a young girl facing these huge obstacles alone, with only a brief explanation, will automatically react in shame and dread. Instead of seeing this process as the "order of things ordained by God" she will view it as something bad, shameful, and dirty. Due to unanswered questions, her self-esteem will plummet, which will in turn heighten her negative emotions. She will stuff down her feelings of sadness and vulnerability, pretending that she is okay, when in reality she is fearful and embarrassed. From this, she may determine that God is fearful and unkind because He was the One who made her this way. Instead of embracing womanhood in a healthy manner, she will dread this process, and like Lisa, wish she wouldn't have been born a girl, or even been born at all. The confusion in an uninformed child can become larger than life and take away her peace.

My prayer is to keep communication open between my daughters and me. *It is a process; not a goal that can be reached once and done.* There is no one perfect way for mothers to approach the topic of puberty with their daughters. You may choose to purchase a book for them, which is just fine. Be sure it is a book with sound teaching on this topic. (*To a Girl of Eleven* is an excellent resource to help you have this talk with your child. I am sure there are other godly publications out there as well. See Resources on page 186.)

By giving them this book to read, or even reading over it with them, you are opening a door of communication that will be beneficial to them all through their teens. After they have read it and returned it to you, be sure to ask them if they understood what they read and if they want to ask you any questions. That way they will feel that you have a vested interest in what they are facing and want to help in any way you can.

You can also try this: tell them to write any questions they may have on a paper and give it to you. You can answer on the paper and through that communicate to them in a way that they will not feel any nervousness or embarrassment. Some children find that an easier way to communicate and that is fine.

You may choose to talk with them, explaining in your own words what will take place in their body in the next few years. That is also appropriate. Don't work yourself up about when exactly to do this, but pray that God will allow an opportunity to arise that will be the perfect time for you to share. You don't need to use a lot of words, but caring enough to warn your daughter and prepare her is your duty. God can give you the grace and the ability to explain it in such a way that will take all the fear out of it. She can maintain her innocence and still trust her mother to be forthright with her.

Above all else, be gentle, calm, and kind. Witness to her that this is not something to be alarmed about, but a very normal part of growing up and becoming the young woman God created her to be.

We must also be careful to caution our daughters about discussing these topics with their peers. It is sad for a parent when a child comes to them with implanted opinions of these things from another child who was misinformed and misguided. I asked my daughter not to talk about it with her friends, because for something like this their mothers will want to be the ones to tell them. It is you, as her mother, that should have the honor of informing your child at the appropriate time.

I also believe that we need to understand that a child need not know all the intricate details of these things. They are still innocent and we can overburden them with too much information. A simple explanation and an openness to questions is sufficient. If they ask something you are not comfortable telling them, do not make them feel ashamed. Simply telling them, "For right now, that may be too hard for you to understand; I will help you understand that when you are older," is a good response when you feel they do not need that information at this time. Generally, if a child does not see that you are trying to hide something from her, but are telling her what she needs to know for now, she will accept this answer.

Corrie Ten Boom talks about a time when she was a little girl and saw the word "rape" in the newspaper while she and her father were walking to the train station. "Father, what does rape mean?" she asked him. He stopped and set down his large trunk.

"Please carry this for me, Corrie," he said.

With puzzlement, she tried to lift the trunk, but it was much too heavy for her to carry. "But it is too heavy for me, Father…" she said.

"And so it would be if I tried to explain to you what rape means. It is too heavy for a little girl to understand. When you are older and can better handle it, I will tell you what this means," her father answered wisely.

And so it is with us and our daughters. We must inform them for their peace of mind and yet not overinform them to the point where we place too heavy a burden on their little backs. Be wise with them, yet kind enough to allow them to still remain innocent and at peace.

Truly, we have a great responsibility! How blessed we are to have the Word of God at our fingertips and His grace and love abiding in our hearts! He is faithful and has not asked more of us than He is willing to supply.

Treasure your daughter; she is God's precious gift to you.

Karla

STAGE 4

Karla flipped through the stack of envelopes as she walked back in the lane. She studied the return address on the small box that had also been in the mailbox. She didn't recognize it. Probably something Dad needed in the shop.

Karla tackled the kitchen windows when she got back to the house. After these she had only the entryway ones to do yet. She noticed something slowing down on the road. It was the truck coming to pick up the weekly load of completed furniture from the shop. Might Steve be the driver?

He was! Karla finished the window she was doing and started the next one vigorously. If she could get this one finished, maybe she could run that small box that had been in the mail out to Dad. She felt slightly embarrassed. If Steve hadn't been the driver, she would not have even thought of taking it out. But he was so good looking and just so nice...

"Mom, I'm going to take this box out to Dad," she called. "Come, Krista. You can go with me."

Karla and Krista walked around the front of the truck and into the shop. Steve and one of the workers were loading furniture. Steve didn't even notice Karla at first, but then he called out a hearty "hello" and pretended to bow. Karla grinned and Krista giggled. Karla left Krista standing there while she walked over to the office with the box for Dad.

Krista wasn't ready to go in, so they stayed awhile to watch. Steve was showing off for their benefit. He grunted and groaned and pretended each chair was terribly heavy. He pulled out a handkerchief and acted as though he were wiping sweat off his forehead. Karla couldn't help noticing the muscles that rippled in his arm, and she knew lifting the furniture was no strain for him. Finally she convinced Krista that they must go back to the house.

Karla finished the windows in a thoughtful mood. Now that her emotions had calmed down, she felt a deep shame. She remembered the week before when Steve had picked up the weekly load and she had been planting potatoes in the patch beside the shop. While he waited on the paperwork for Dad he had walked over and inspected her job. He had told her how he and his siblings had planted potatoes years ago. He had demonstrated how they measured the space between potatoes with their feet. He told her, with plenty of exaggeration, how sore his back had become after planting rows of potatoes.

Karla had felt uncomfortable. But she told herself that he was just a lonely man, and that she couldn't help it if he had stopped to chat a bit. But she also knew that she had enjoyed the attention too much. She hadn't thought it affected her, but maybe it had.

ooooooooooooooooooooooooooooooooooooooooooooooooooooooooooooooooooooooo

Karla finished the dishes and turned to wipe the table. Dad was still sitting at his place sipping his coffee. He was looking at her thoughtfully. In a rush, the uncomfortable feelings flooded her again. She had brushed them off in the midst of supper preparations and cleanup, but they hadn't dissolved.

Karla tossed for a while that night. She longed to go tell Mom everything, but Mom was already in bed. Karla knew Mom wouldn't mind being awakened, but still she didn't want to bother her. Then with a jolt she remembered the girl from the family who used to be their neighbors. They had moved several years ago, but she still remembered the trauma the family went through when their seventeen-year-old daughter left home to live with a man who had worked for them.

Seventeen. In a little over a year, Karla would be the same age. She shuddered. She couldn't imagine leaving home to live with a man, but—

Karla heard someone go to the kitchen. She heard the oven door opening. Oh yes, the yogurt. They had put it in the oven to culture, and she and Mom had both forgotten to move it to the refrigerator at bedtime. Apparently Mom had remembered now. Almost before she knew what she was doing, Karla was out of bed and on her way to the kitchen.

Mom heard her coming. "Do you need something?"

"Well," Karla hesitated. She got a drink of water. "I wanted to talk—uh, do you have time now?"

"I do," Mom said. "What is on your mind?"

"Uh, well," Karla started and then stopped. She tried again. "I shouldn't have gone to the shop like I did this afternoon."

Mom said gently, "Was it because of Steve?"

Karla felt relieved that Mom understood. She wiped a tear as she nodded.

"Dad and I were talking about it," Mom said in such a caring tone that more tears came. Karla reached for a tissue.

"Did you know Steve is a divorced man?" Mom asked.

Karla gasped. Steve divorced? That turned on a whole different light in her mind. Suddenly the thought that she had felt attracted to him repulsed her. A divorced man!

"Dad said it would be best if you don't come to the shop when Steve comes to pick up furniture," Mom said. "He is too friendly with women.

"Karla, you are a young woman," Mom went on. "You need to be reserved around men. It's normal to feel an attraction for men.

God designed it that way, but that attraction needs to be carefully controlled until marriage. Controlling it means being careful with your words and actions around men—not flirting, in other words—but most of all you need to control your thoughts."

Karla nodded.

Mom continued, "The Bible says to keep ourselves pure, and that means not only actions and words, it means our thoughts also. Don't let yourself dream or think about a man. It will lead to many disappointments and problems."

Karla nodded again, and in a voice that was somewhat strained she asked, "How—how do you not think about men?"

Mom sighed. "I wish there was an easy answer, but there isn't. Fill your mind with Bible verses and songs instead. It's a continual battle, because Satan does not want us to control our thoughts."

Mother and daughter were silent for a bit, and then Mom asked gently, "Do you read the Bible and pray regularly?"

Karla nodded, but seemed uncertain. Mom waited.

"I do, but," Karla hesitated, "sometimes I just can't keep my mind on what I'm reading or praying about. I guess that's not controlling my thoughts very well…"

"I know what you mean," Mom said. "It's something I struggle with too. It's another area Satan will certainly attack us, because if he can get us to think about something else instead of what we are reading or praying, well—then he has done what he wanted to do. It might help to keep a notebook and write down a verse each day that means a lot to you. Or even write down your prayer. It helps you to stay focused."

"I should try that," Karla remarked, and then all was silent again for a bit.

"There's another thing that I wanted to talk to you about," Mom began again. "We appreciate that you are making your dresses modestly. That is another thing that is very important for a girl to do. You know, men have to work just as hard as women to keep their thought life pure, and when they see a woman dressed in form-fitting clothes, can you guess how that makes them struggle? And the sobering thought about that is, if you dress in a way that causes a man to struggle, is it only his fault? Would God hold only him accountable for those thoughts?"

"But how…" Karla paused. "How am I supposed to do all that right? It's, it's—hard!"

"I know," Mom said. "Living for God isn't easy.

"Living for God isn't easy," she repeated. "But it is possible. Instead of looking ahead and feeling overwhelmed because of the future, focus only on today. Live for God one day at a time. And if you fail—no, *when* you fail—because you will; no one is perfect—then remember that God *wants* to forgive you. You only have to sincerely ask Him to."

Karla smiled at her mother. The load inside was gone. She knew she would be able to sleep now. She felt a renewed desire to serve God. And even though she couldn't have put it into words, her love and respect for her mother was strengthened.

Lisa Lisa was gathering the ingredients to mix up bread dough when Dad hurried through the door. "I need some bolts and things at the hardware store," he said. "Here's the list. Can one of you go?"

Mom turned to Lisa, but she was already washing her hands and brushing off her dress. "While you are going anyway, stop at the grocery store for ingredients to make granola." Mom counted out and handed Lisa the cash she would need.

Lisa hurried for the door, but Mom called her back. "Put something on besides flip-flops," she exclaimed.

"Why?" Lisa demanded with a drawn-out sigh. She made no attempt to hide her irritation. "It's finally warm today."

"Because I told you to," Mom said, and turned away to indicate that the conversation was over.

Lisa stood still for a moment, silently fuming. For a few seconds, she was very tempted to go in flip-flops anyway. But finally, she stomped to her room for other footwear.

Lisa was still upset a few minutes later on her way to the store. "I'm sixteen years old! A person should be allowed to make some of their own choices at that age." But then her thoughts traveled ahead of her to the hardware store. Her countenance changed and she smiled, a smug little smile. "I hope Chad is at work today."

Dad needed parts regularly, and being the homebody he was, he preferred to send someone else. It was just this spring that Lisa was allowed to go herself, and she had soon come to enjoy the job. Really, it was because of Chad that she was so willing to run Dad's errands, but she was careful to hide that fact from her parents.

Only one other customer was in the store, and Chad grinned and waved at Lisa. "Howdy," he said, in the casual manner that Lisa had come to enjoy. "What brings you in? Me, I suppose?" He guffawed at his own joke.

Lisa grinned back and waved a hand at him as if annoyed. "Parts for Dad," she said.

Chad pretended to be disappointed. "I could have known. You came for your dad instead of for me. Well, now that he's not here, but I am, can I help you?"

Lisa giggled and pulled the list from her pocket. She laid it on the counter for Chad, but instead of reaching for it like usual, he came around the end of the counter to stand beside her. Then slowly, he ran his finger down the list of items Dad needed.

Lisa's breath caught in her throat, and she felt her face getting hot. Feelings—the feelings she was starting to enjoy since she knew

Chad—surged within her. She glanced around. Where was the other customer?

He was talking to someone back in the corner. Chad turned to go to the bolt bins and saw her looking around. He winked. "Come along. Dan is keeping him occupied."

While Chad picked out and bagged the bolts, he kept up a stream of conversation. Like usual. Lisa had felt guilty at first when she and Chad talked, but she had persuaded herself that he was just a friendly man and he was only doing his job. Subconsciously she noticed the other customer pay for his items and walk out. Dan went into the office and shut the door. She and Chad were alone in the store.

A guilty feeling nudged her, but she shoved it away. She'd deal with it later. Right now Chad wanted to know what she had done that weekend, and she told him. About the volleyball game. About the walk the girls had taken. About their plans for the next weekend.

She followed Chad around the store as he collected what Dad wanted, and they chattered on and on. Chad had such a way of making her feel special. She wondered if he treated every customer this way, or only her. She took note of his informal, but neat clothes. She liked how expressive his eyes were. She noticed his cologne.

Finally she was walking out the door, and Chad was calling after her, "Come back soon, Lisa." She checked the time. She gasped. Was it really? She had been in there a half hour!

Now she would have to hurry. Dad would be waiting on his parts. She rushed the whole way home, and plopped the bag of items on the shop table. Dad wasn't there.

She hurried toward the house and met him coming out. "About time," he said. "I thought you must have taken the parts into the house. Where are they?"

"In the shop," Lisa said.

Mom looked surprised when she walked into the house. "Where is the oatmeal for the granola?" she asked.

Lisa stopped. The oatmeal! She had totally forgotten.

Mom looked annoyed and then bewildered. "You mean you forgot? Where were you so long if you weren't at the grocery store? I told Dad that's why you were gone so long."

Lisa scrambled for an answer. "I don't know," she said. "It was such a nice day. I guess I was enjoying being outside." She rushed on. She had to distract Mom. "I saw the first daffodils blooming in Martha's flowerbed."

Mom sighed. "I wish you would learn to be dependable," she said. "Well, just make a small batch of granola with the oatmeal we have. You'll have to make more next week then."

Lisa turned in relief. That had been close enough. She would have to be more careful after this.

◇◇

That evening as Lisa dutifully read a chapter in her Bible, guilt flooded her again. She should tell Mom and Dad that she'd rather not go to the hardware store again. She knew she shouldn't be so friendly to Chad, but he was so likable. She'd just enjoy chatting with him now and then, but she would be careful. Round and round her mind went until she had herself convinced that nothing was wrong.

She went to bed, but there was no deep peace in her heart. There was a vague discomfort that she couldn't quite define. An emptiness—a hole or something. She didn't know what it was, and she didn't know how to figure it out. She knew it had to do with her heart. And God. Life was so confusing. But there was Chad—he made everything feel good again.

The next morning Lisa did not feel rested. She felt guilty

whenever she remembered her dream about Chad. She and Chad had been on a boat in the middle of a huge lake. And all her friends had been watching from the shores and she could tell they were jealous of her. Chad had leaned toward her, and then she could feel herself waking up. She had tried to stay asleep. She wanted the dream to finish, but it didn't. It had floated away and left the empty feeling there again.

Lisa worked at packing lunches for the scholars. Her brother walked by. "Ugh, apples," he said. He looked into his lunch. "And bologna sandwiches again. Can't you pack something good for once?"

"Get out of here," Lisa exploded, and shoved him.

"Owww," he said loudly, looking in Mom's direction.

Mom sighed. "Could you two please stop that," she said. "Daniel, go get ready for school. Lisa, really now…"

Lisa clenched her teeth and turned away. The day was starting out like usual.

Her mood improved when Mom sent her to hang out the laundry after breakfast. She had not liked the job when she was younger, but now she had come to enjoy it. She was all by herself and she could let her thoughts roam where they wished. Lately they traveled to the hardware store. She savored her memories of Chad and concocted possible future scenes. She knew she would feel dirty and guilty when she was done, but she would push off those nasty feelings as long as possible. If only—if only Dad would need some parts again today.

Finally, there was no more wet laundry waiting. Feeling suddenly morose, Lisa trudged toward the house. She passed the sandbox and the row of daffodils beside it. They were nearly in bloom. She remembered how she had mentioned Martha's daffodils to Mom yesterday.

It was symbolic almost. That Martha's daffodils were in bloom and theirs weren't. Big deal that Martha's were on the south side of the house and theirs were on the northeast. Things just went well for that family—Karla's family. They all seemed so happy. Lisa knew that Karla and her mom were good friends. She could just tell. She knew it was that way for some of her other friends too.

She felt no connection like that herself. Mom wasn't unkind—not really—she was just happiest if left to herself. Though she couldn't have put it into words, she longed for things to be different. But it was just part of the emptiness inside. She supposed it would always be there.

ooooooooooooooooooooooooooooooooooooooooooooooooooooooooooooooooooooooo

Remember the feelings? The up and down roller coaster of emotions that seem to follow you through your teenage days? The wayward thoughts? The shameful feelings? Oh, the turmoil that can build up within the heart of a teenage girl…

Lisa and Karla were both struggling in the same way. Becoming aware of the attention of a man and the feelings that accompany that, all the while unsure of those feelings and their intensity.

The desire to be especially noticed by someone of the other sex is very normal. To the teenager who is experiencing it, though, it feels anything but normal. The heart pounds, the cheeks redden, and the eyes just can't seem to stop looking… Many times, during waking hours, the thoughts turn that direction seemingly unbidden.

A young girl can go weeks ruminating on a single kind word, smile, or deed of a man she admires.

As earlier stated, it is all very normal. And if we as mothers are honest and look back, we can surely tap into our own struggles as a teen and use that to be a comfort and a source of stability to our daughter in these rocky years.

Karla's mother had been paying enough attention to her daughter that she realized her infatuation with Steve before Karla mentioned feeling bad about it. Their communication was such that Karla wanted to talk to her mother about it, even if she was ashamed. Through that, Karla had her eyes opened to who Steve really was and was able to lay those feelings to rest. Had she never talked about it with her mother, she may have gone on looking for ways to chat with him and feeding that desire within to be noticed, in an unhealthy way.

Again, communication is a process, starting when a child is small. They do not just one day decide to communicate with their parents. It has to be nurtured throughout their childhood. As a mother, showing an interest in them when they are five and listening to them is the way to start that cycle of communication that will help them be more comfortable to share when they are fifteen.

For a teenage girl to know that, yes, it is a normal process of growing up to desire to be noticed by someone special, will help them feel more secure. Although the desire is there, the timing needs to be God's. If they can confide in you, you can direct them to the Lord when their feelings want to run away with them. You also have life experience and know that it takes much more than emotions to build a lasting relationship. Just being able to share with Mom can help to place those feelings in the proper place.

Lisa's feelings were fed so much in her mind that it was affecting her life in an unhealthy way. She was giddy, irresponsible, and moody. (Another very normal part of being a teenager, but not a necessary one.) But most of all, she was feeling alone. She interpreted that to mean she was better left alone. (Very dangerous for a teenager.) Who could she talk to about the guilt she felt when she recognized her inappropriate behavior? Her situation compounded her feelings and she looked with envy at Karla's life...

Young girls are very quick to pick up on a "good relationship" between a mother and daughter. Why is that? Is it not because they long for that very thing for themselves? They desire to be open with you—after all, you are their mother! If they cannot communicate with you, they will fill that empty place (that you are supposed to fill) with something else. Sadly, that need is often met in unhealthy ways.

As godly mothers, we want to teach our daughters reserve and restraint. If we simply say to them, "Don't act like that!" or "Don't make your dresses so tight!" we place them on the defensive and make them feel worse for those feelings than they already do. Like Karla's mother, we need to explain to them why we don't behave in certain ways. Why we clothe ourselves in modesty. Why we are careful when talking with men or boys. Why we try to guard our thoughts and feelings so that they don't carry us away into bad decisions.

I commend Karla's mother for admitting that she struggles too. Being open with our daughters and letting them see that we are not perfect, but need the help of God to remain pure in thoughts and in actions, is vital. To not portray ourselves as having accomplished all, but that we are in this together gives them an accurate picture of the Christian life. If we stand "above" them scolding and shaming them to behave the way we think they should, we will hinder their relationship with Christ. How can they see a loving Father as an authority figure, if the mother who says she loves and worships Him, is condemning and unapproachable?

I plead with you mothers not to neglect your teenage daughters. Listen to them. Read between the lines to try to understand what they haven't said. Teach them in love. Pray for wisdom to understand the turmoil of feelings and needs. Pray that God will give you unfailing love when they seem most unlovable.

The Scriptures say in Proverbs 29:15: *The rod and reproof give wisdom: but a child left to himself bringeth his mother to shame.* Your daughter will bring you much shame if she is left to make decisions by herself. Many of her decisions will be based on feelings. You need to help her see the truth of the matter, minus her feelings.

There are many, many stories out there about young women who have been wooed into relationships that were ungodly. Although your daughter will have to make her own choices (you cannot make them all for her), be there for her, to listen and to really hear.

Most of all: *pray for her*. God knows your daughter and her needs better than you ever will, and He is big enough to fill in the gaps left by your failure. With God's help you can lead your daughter safely into womanhood. ✸

Layers of Prayer
Amy Schlabach

Dear Lord, I haven't time to spend
Long hours on my knees,
For I am a busy mother...
So help me, O Lord, please,
To pray all through my daily work;
I want to do my part,
And lift my loved ones up to God
In the closet of my heart.

COME!
STAND in the LIGHT
Anonymous

T he crowd of young boys clustered in the shadows were
enjoying a high time. Church was over and a dark corner was
the perfect spot for wrestling, jostling, and joking. But wait, who
comes here?

The young pastor bounded down the church steps with zeal
matching his nature. Approaching the group of boys, he spoke
enthusiastically. "Boys, come stand in the light! The light is much
better than darkness!"

The boys sheepishly abandoned their shadowy corner and headed
to a well-lit spot. Under exposure of light, conduct improved.

∞∞

I was a young girl, observing the above incident from the sidelines.
But today, as a young bishop's wife, the memory of the pastor's
reaction to a less than ideal situation still blesses me. The pastor
could have sidled quietly by, casting sad, sidelong glances at "those

naughty boys," and gone home burdened. He could have made a mental note to speak to the "irresponsible parents," admonishing them to set their children straight. He could have approached the boys with a condemning, better-than-thou, you-listen-here tone of voice. Instead, he used straightforward, personable, and clear invitation.

I wonder how many young folks have fallen away because we adults skirt issues. A sister from a Mennonite church recently shared, "I personally think we have lost more youth from the church here because of not squarely asking them how it's going than for any other reason. Most, if not all our youth who left here, left with the baggage of immoral garbage. It breaks my heart to think of it. There is only one youth boy left. My husband often asks him how it's going and keeps him accountable. I don't know if his dad or the ministers do or not. It's not a subject spoken of a whole lot."

Let's not kid ourselves into thinking that immoral practices are all "out there" in the world. Another young sister from a conservative church shared, "Out of the group of girls I grew up with, at least 75% of us had the problem of self-abuse or issues of girls with girls. I look back and feel so terrible… I *taught* one of those girls how to do it… and I have a passion for this subject. I think it is more common than we know. So address it!"

We pray for our young people to be pure. We observe our youth, drawing conclusions and forming concerns. We teach proper dress codes and appropriate conduct. But, have they ever been given the gift of clear teaching on purity in a comfortable atmosphere, where they find out there is a right and good way to talk about these things? Are they kindly being asked if they have failed in purity issues?

We feel blessed to have the example and direction of a senior bishop who was upfront, yet personable. Sitting in on meetings he chaired, we were amazed and blessed at his ability to put someone at ease, yet dig deep and thoroughly when getting down to the matter at hand. I can still picture him chuckling at my newly ordained husband's obvious trepidation when told to ask a recently converted boy in church if he had moral issues in the past.

We are still young in the ministry and look forward to learning much more. But I will share just a few things we are learning.

Be personal and personable. The apostle Paul lamented that there are thousands of instructors, yet few fathers. An instructor imparts knowledge—cold, hard facts. The truth may reach the head, but hardly the heart. A true shepherd carries his flock on his heart. Loving concern for those under our care moves us to reach their hearts. There is no quick or pat recipe for accomplishing this. As parents, pastors, and pastors' wives we often bumble and are unsure of ourselves. But our inexperience is no excuse for omission. Go with a heart of love and humility, pick a relaxed atmosphere and attitude, and God will guide you. Never give the impression that you are up on a rung above them. One young sister told of sharing a struggle with a pastor's wife. She was surprised and blessed when the pastor's wife exclaimed, "Oh, I've struggled with that too! But let me tell you how my husband helped me; perhaps it can help you too." Even when you cannot really relate with the struggles they are sharing, be caring and compassionate.

Never act horrified when they begin opening their hearts and ugly worms start popping up. When inwardly shocked, act outwardly calm. This revealing is exciting! God's Spirit is beginning a major clean-up process!

Teach. Be clear in your teaching. My husband's preaching on impurity nearly causes my ears to burn as he exposes the terribleness of Satan's lies in the form of impurity. He gets practical, bringing it down to daily temptations and thoughts. He does not speak of impurity as being something "out there," but recognizes it as a temptation we're daily bombarded with, and which we need to cry out to God to remain free of.

Ideally, parents should be the ones to teach children about "the birds and bees," along with other teaching on purity. Sadly, many parents do not. My husband checks up on fathers in the church, to see if they are talking with their boys. I have held classes with girls from non-Christian or struggling homes, sometimes in a group and sometimes individually. We study issues pertinent to girls, among them purity. When held in a group, I have them answer the study questions privately, writing out their answers. Reading the answers they hand in are very revealing; they seem freer to write about things hard to discuss.

Do girls who have "seen it all" still need teaching? Yes. While going through *God's Will for My Body* with a young girl from an ungodly home, she repeatedly exclaimed on what a blessing it is to learn about such things from a godly perspective instead of the dirty context she had known.

Provide clear, loving direction. While relationship is important, young folks need more than a buddy; they need a leader. When my husband asked a lighthearted young sister to stop reading romance books, I was sure she would be upset with us. Not so. Even though her mom read romance, she conscientiously abstained and later thanked us for our direction.

Inquire. God taught me this again. For some unexplainable reason, I sometimes wondered if a certain single sister was victorious in personal purity. I felt bad for even wondering. She was very spiritual by all appearances, and much appreciated in the church. Wouldn't it be a disgrace to ask her? So I brushed it aside. Time went on. An issue arose where it became obvious that she had her emotions tied up in a boy, only to have hopes shattered. While visiting with her on the matter, I decided I might as well ask about personal purity. She was not victorious. She had repented, confessing it to God, but repeatedly fell. She did not know if she should go beyond confessing it to God or not and had prayed that if she should make it public, that God would send someone to ask her. I trembled to think of how close I came to not heeding the Spirit.

Don't pour concrete on your feelings, but do pay attention to them. In a church I attended for a time, there were two brethren who I wondered about. Everything looked good on the surface and I could not lay a finger on why I felt the way I did, except that both were very shifty-eyed. "That's just their nature," I assured myself. Both were later convicted as sexual offenders. A sister who boarded one of them later told me, "If you ever feel uneasy about someone, pay attention." She too felt uneasy about the young man but, like me, thought it was senseless imaginations. Years later she and her husband made the sickening discovery that this young man, a church member in voluntary service, had been abusing their boys.

Inspire. The best way to avoid a pitfall is by staying on a straight path and being totally enthralled with it. Be clear on teaching about the devil's horrible counterfeit, but be just as straightforward on the beauty of God's genuine design. Inspire awe at His perfect plan. Be an example of the true and the lovely. Be discreet, but not embarrassed about His awesome plan. I love to hear preachers share a glimpse of their beautiful marriage, or an example of how their wife has blessed them.

Show affection. This may sound counter-productive, but it is not. I am not referring to erotic kissing and caressing between parents; I am speaking of children seeing a quick hug, or kiss-on-the-cheek kind of thing. Children knowing they may walk beside, but not between Daddy and Mommy. Children giggling over finding clothespins where Daddy wrote love notes to Mommy. I think even their hearing, "Don't touch that snack; it's a special treat for when Daddy and I are alone," makes them glad inside. A young boy said, "When Daddy comes home and gives Mommy a kiss, it makes me so happy I hardly know what to do with myself." Why? It gives a needed sense of security. They are seeing God's perfect design of true love lived out in daily life. Children living with the security of the real thing are much less susceptible to Satan's counterfeit.

"Confess your faults one to another, and pray one for another,

that ye may be healed." When we sin we hate exposure, for we know that exposure is a death blow to part of us. Is simply confessing a sin to the Lord enough? In situations we have observed, it seems true or lasting victory is rarely found when an individual only confesses their failure to the Lord. Churches vary in how public they go with confessions. Our church has found it strengthening to confess faults, sins, and temptations publicly, even personal impurity. Pastors or their wives can help the individual decide on an appropriate way to describe the sin. My husband feels that declaring the sin is needful, as opposed to a vague, "I've had some struggles and failed." Before communion we all share our testimonies publicly. The devil would whisper in our ear that others will be horrified if we are totally honest, but the opposite is true. I rarely feel such a strong sense of love and unity as that which permeates the church immediately following those special times of sharing.

Pray for sin to be revealed. My father, a church leader, repeatedly prayed that God would reveal if there is any hidden sin in the church, and God honored his request. It would be so much easier to look the other way and poke our head in the sand. From little up we have been taught to mind our own business. As adults, we begin to realize that we are our brother's keeper. As parents, the impact of our accountability weighs on us. And those who are called to the ministry waken to the fact that "digging in others' business" is, actually, now their business. We shrink from it, especially in cases where the digging is not appreciated. But God will reveal sin if we honestly ask Him to.

∞∞

God is light. As we live under His beam of exposure we have fellowship one with another. Together we extend welcoming hands to those in shadowy corners enthusiastically inviting, "Come, stand in the light!"

CULTIVATING A RELATIONSHIP OF GOLD

A Counselor's Wife

Developing a warm, loving relationship is one of the best defenses against impurity.

Juanita muttered under her breath when she heard the baby fussing. She was busy. She had baking to do. The floor needed sweeping. She grabbed the bottle of Tylenol and gave her little one a good dose. There now. She should sleep for several hours with that medicine.

The baby grew. Although Juanita fed her children, she did not seem to really care about them. She sent them away from where she was working. She didn't talk to them about little children things. She didn't talk to them about God.

Juanita probably never thought about how many opportunities she was missing in her children's lives. Her children grew up, but they missed out on the close relationship that God intended for mothers and their children to have.

As these children grow old enough to wonder about their developing sexuality, who will they ask about it? Certainly not their mother if there is no relationship established.

What can mothers do to open the doors of communication with their children? Is it possible for children to feel so close to their mothers that the children will ask Mom those private questions, instead of having whispered secrets with a friend in a dark corner?

The very best time to start developing a close relationship with your children is before they are born. Unborn babies need the nurture of love from their parents. Pray for your unborn one. God provides the love for you to pass on to your little one.

A newborn infant who is loved and wanted has a wonderful foundation for a good relationship with her mother as she grows up. That relationship is like gold for both you and your children. It becomes more valuable with every passing year.

∞∞

Unlike Juanita, Marla spent time with her children. She enjoyed talking to them as she worked. She often talked about God and showed them the wonders of His creation. The brilliant stars, the glowing moon, or a pretty flower were all things to admire together and thank God for. Often Marla and her children sang songs or she told them a story.

Is it any wonder that her children loved her? They were happy children and obedient. They were secure.

One day as Marla bathed little Kayla, she noticed Kayla playing with her bottom.

"No, Kayla," Marla said firmly, and pulled Kayla's hand away from her bottom. "I don't want you to play with your body."

Kayla looked up at her mommy, her black eyes serious. "Play?" she asked.

Marla breathed a prayer for wisdom. How could she explain this so that little Kayla would understand?

"Who made you, Kayla?"

Kayla nodded her head solemnly. "God did."

"God loves you, Kayla."

Kayla smiled, and a sparkle crept back into her eyes.

"God doesn't want you to play with your body, Kayla. And He doesn't want other people to play with it either." Marla wrapped her daughter in a towel and sat down, holding her close. "If anyone ever plays with your body, then you come tell me. Can you do that, Kayla?"

Kayla nodded. "Kayla tell Mommy," she murmured.

As Marla dried her precious little girl, she knew the teaching would have to be repeated. Little ones forget. She slipped clean underwear and a dress on her daughter. "Oh, God," her heart whispered, "help me to be alert to her needs as she grows. I long for her to always have a clean heart, too!"

∘∘

Teaching modesty

Are diapers important for babies? Must little girls wear panties? Must little boys wear pants?

Covering our children's bottom is good hygiene, but it also serves a deeper purpose. It teaches modesty. We do well to teach our little ones to be covered. Nakedness is shameful (Revelation 3:18).

Little girls may get sore bottoms or even vaginal yeast infections. Be alert and investigate if she seems to be uncomfortable or itchy. Meet her physical needs. Make her feel loved and cared about.

Another area in which to be watchful is in bathing your little boys and girls at the same time. Don't leave boys and girls alone together, undressed. Maybe about age two would be a good time to separate the sexes for bath time. Unsupervised and undressed is an open door for mischief to start. Teach them not to play with each other's private parts.

It is best to have separate bedrooms for your boys and girls. But if the beds are all in one room, perhaps you can put curtains around the beds to provide some privacy. Have the children always change clothes in a separate, private room, like the bathroom.

Is their nightwear modest?

Parents, be private with your love life. Children should daily see affection between parents, but not sensuousness. They should not be able to hear your intimate times.

Teach your little girls modesty. I was impressed to see our two-year-old granddaughter lying on the floor playing, and all the while her legs stayed straight and her dress down. "How did you accomplish that?" I asked her mom. "By keeping after her!" she replied. Good for Mom! That was more than I accomplished with ours. Another suggestion is buying short leggings. Her upper legs will be covered in case of unintended exposure. One sister makes bloomers, which are also more modest than regular panties. Be careful in choosing underwear. Some colors and decorations show through a dress. We do well to be careful with sheer dress fabrics. Use slips that almost reach the dress hem. Get your daughter to stand in a lighted doorway. Does she need a thicker slip?

Modesty goes deeper than dress. It affects the way we act, talk, and laugh. It affects how we walk and the postures we adopt. We have the privilege of helping our daughters know how to conduct themselves modestly. What a huge favor we do to all the men and boys who see us, if we carry ourselves in a spirit of humility and modesty, not trying to get attention. I cherish 1 Peter 3:1-4 and 1 Tim. 2:9-15.

The meek and quiet spirit is very valuable to God. Ask Him for wisdom to teach your daughters these traits He loves. And remember, the best teaching you can do carries no value without your own good example.

Avoiding sexual abuse

Another important way you can safeguard your children is by knowing where they are, who they are with, and what they are playing. Check on them frequently. This is even more important when playmates are of mixed genders, or from ungodly backgrounds. Do not feel bad requiring them to stay within eyesight and earshot if you have reservations. Children should not be allowed to play behind closed doors. Boredom often leads to trouble. Never assume all is well; check on them.

Suppose your child was the instigator in inappropriate exploration. Is an admonition enough or do they need a spanking? You know your child. Two things seem vital here: 1. They must get the message that sexual explorations are wrong. 2. They need to feel "cleared" and free from guilt when your session is done.

Fathers need to have a healthy relationship with their daughters. Children find security when Daddy plays with them and holds them. A good-night kiss on the cheek is a nice bedtime ritual. However, many relatives and neighbors have crossed the line from a healthy relationship to a hurtful one. Symptoms of sexual abuse vary greatly. Wringing hands, nervousness, unexplained crying, or other behavioral changes may be indicators. One four-year-old suddenly started having bathroom issues. Her busy mother found a private moment and slowly extracted the horrifying truth from her fearful daughter. It was her grandfather who was molesting her and told her to not tell.

Sexual abuse happens. Let's do all we can as mothers to prevent that sin. Teach your children to immediately tell you if anyone touches or asks to see their private parts. (They will often be threatened to not tell.) An abused child who feels protected has much less trauma and guilt to deal with than one who tries to bury the hurt and confusion and doesn't report what happened to her.

But we need balance. We need not fear a bear behind every bush. Maybe nightmares are a simple calcium deficiency. Pray for wisdom. Ask a seasoned mother for advice. Get help. It is your responsibility to protect your children.

Cultivate openness with your daughters.

I was visiting a home one day, and the 4-year-old asked her mommy a sex-related question. The embarrassed mother exclaimed, "Be quiet!" Poor girlie! She walked away hurt and bewildered. Her mother could have given her a simple answer in front of her visitor, and told her she would explain more later. That would have helped to develop that golden relationship. Instead, her response drove her child away and closed an emotional door. What a shame! A calm answer could have opened the door for future conversations.

You, Mother, have the responsibility to talk to your girls about sexual things. If you don't tell them, they will learn the facts sooner than you wish, in ways you wish they would not. It is far better if they hear the teaching from you. This fortifies them to respond properly when they are exposed to sexual talk from others. Hearing the facts whispered to them by peers builds insecurity in the child. Why? The information is usually presented in a vulgar form, and not accurate. How much better it is to hear of such things from their parents, presented in a wholesome, godly perspective! Even if you feel very inadequate in knowing how to explain things, go ahead and do it. A stumbling, imperfect conversation will be much better than none at all. Your daughter will know that you cared enough to put forth the effort to teach her, and she will honor you for it. And do relax. If you are uptight, your daughter will get the message that this is a scary subject and will not be as free with questions. The book *God's Will for My Body* can be helpful to go through with your child.

∞∞∞

Here is a true story about a 4-year-old, and how her mother taught her age-appropriate facts.

Monica

One day Monica accompanied her mother to town. They parked the car and headed down the street, hand in hand. Mommy pointed to the hospital they were passing. "Do you see that building, Monica?"

"Yes, it is big!"

Mommy turned the corner, as they headed to the dentist's office. "You were born in that hospital, Monica." Her voice was sweet and special.

Monica turned to look at her mother. "I was?!" Her eyes sparkled, and she gazed back at the hospital. "I was born there." She repeated it in awed tone. "Mommy, where was I before I was born?"

Mommy breathed a quick prayer for wisdom. Was now the time to teach Monica a little bit more? She smiled at her wide-eyed daughter. "Monica, God made a special place for babies to grow until they are born. You were in that special place. You were inside my tummy."

Monica's eyes grew even bigger. "Inside your tummy?! But Mommy! How did I get there?"

Mommy smiled again, and her hand stroked Monica's hair affectionately. "You started out very tiny. I'll tell you more about that when you get older and you can understand it better. But you started out very tiny, and you grew and grew, and when you were big enough, you were born."

Monica stared back at the hospital again, then turned to her mother, wonder and surprise in her voice. "How did I come out of your tummy?"

Mommy had a flashback to her own childhood and her misconceptions. For many years, she had thought that doctors always cut a tummy open to get a baby out. All the questions she had asked her elders were skillfully evaded. Birth was a mystery to her until finally, when she was 12 years old, she happened to see a cow give birth. That had answered many questions for her. She did not want Monica to experience the years of confusion and unanswered questions she herself had gone through. Nor did she want to explain too much. After all, Monica was only four!

"God, I need Your help!" her prayer flew heavenward. Out loud, she said kindly, "God made a special way for babies to be born. When you are older I will explain more."

"Did the doctor cut your tummy open to get me out?"

"No. But sometimes doctors have to do that."

Monica bounced along, her eyes glowing, her face happy.

"Monica, do you remember what a 'secret' is?"

Monica nodded.

"What we just talked about is our secret. If you want to talk more about it, you may talk to Daddy or me anytime. But I don't want you to talk to any of your little friends or to your cousins about being born or about being in my tummy. Can you remember that?"

Monica's eyes grew solemn as she nodded. "What shall I do if they talk to me about it?"

"Just don't say anything, and come and tell me."

Monica nodded.

"Let's go into the dentist office now," Mommy said. "I need to pay a bill."

As they walked toward the office door, Mommy felt a little hand slip into her own. Mommy looked down. Monica's little face was upturned, and she gave Mommy a smile of wonder and deep contentment.

∞∞∞

Not all children will ask questions like Monica did. That made it easier for her mother. Whether or not your children ask questions, you have the awesome privilege of teaching your children these sacred facts, bit by bit, in a wholesome way that inspires reverence for God. How rich your children will be if you teach them! How much better than learning in a shameful, secretive way that leaves them guilty and ashamed, as if sex were something dirty.

Remember the golden relationship? Can you see it glowing in Monica's story? Every constructive daily interaction makes that relationship grow more precious, more golden. As your children grow older and you continue to teach them little by little, their confidence in you grows. They will feel secure and protected, and will trust you with their questions and confusions when those difficult teenage years come. Stay in tune with your children. Listen to them. Discover what is in their heart. Learn what they are thinking. Stay close to them.

The age of girls' development varies. Sometime between the ages of 9 and 11 is probably about the right time to talk to her about how her body will change. Tell her that sometime in the next year or so, she may notice that her breasts feel a little funny, or sore. Maybe they will feel hard, and they will start to grow. Tell her this is normal and a special part of growing up.

Soon you will be telling her about more changes. She will need to know about pubic and armpit hair growth. You will explain to her about the monthly cycle. Show her what to do when she gets her first period. Your positive attitude will help her be positive too, even though there may be some discomfort associated with her cycle.

Be a real mother. Talk to your daughters. We have all heard of the tragic teen pregnancies. Your daughter needs you to tell her how and why pregnancy happens. Informed, loved, secure young girls are much less vulnerable to the lustful advances of men and boys.

Do not expect others to take care of talking to your daughter about purity issues or the changes in her body; your daughter needs *you*. She needs that closeness with you, her mother. She needs the security of knowing that you care enough to talk to her, even though you are not able to explain it perfectly. Both of you need the openness, the trust, that such wholesome conversation brings. Ask God for wisdom as to exactly when, where, and how to open such a conversation. You will want privacy. Remind your daughter that these talks are not subject matter to be discussed with peers. Invite her to come to you with questions.

As you feel the timing and her maturity developing, explain intimacy to her. You will tell her that in marriage, sex is a beautiful thing between parents who love each other. Hebrews 13:4 tells us that marriage is honorable. Tell her that outside of marriage, sex is wrong, and results in much shame and guilt. Help her to understand that holding hands and physical contact with a male may well lead her to a physical union that is wrong.

How can we prepare our intermediate daughter for the attention from boys or men that stir brand-new feelings in her? As she enters adolescence, she may start flirting without realizing what she is doing, nor why. Help her to understand that as her hormones develop, she will notice boys in a new way. She may catch herself doing things to attract their attention. Those glances or giggles, those big smiles, are flirting. Prepare her for those temptations, and encourage her to practice reserve around men, whether married or single.

Inspire her to invest these adolescent years well. It is a once-in-a-lifetime phase to grow spiritually, mature emotionally, and learn the many things she will need later in life.

Another thing to teach her is the dangers in body language. The way a girl walks or carries herself can be very suggestive, or it can be modest. Her clothing should be modest also. Her legs should be covered, her dresses loose fitting with modest necklines. Her hair should be combed modestly and adequately covered (1 Cor. 11). She needs to be aware that her conduct and dress can make it very hard for Christian men to have clean thoughts. Conversely, her modesty and reserve can be an inspiration to all who see her.

Purity is a priceless virtue, and is becoming increasingly rare in today's world. Help your daughter to value purity, and to safely guard her own. Paint a word picture for her of the joy and blessing of a godly marriage. Help her to resolve deep in her heart to reserve her body for her husband. What more priceless gift than purity can a couple give each other on their wedding day?

Coach her along as you see her maturing. Keep your relationship close as she walks through those teenage years. Go the second mile and talk to her about the things that interest her. If she feels loved and secure and wanted in your home, her heart won't be starved for the attentions of a boy.

When Lily was 16, her peers began connecting her name to a mature young man from church. She really did admire him. He was dedicated to God and had many desirable qualities. The teasing wore her down, and even though she deeply yearned for God's will in her life, she slipped into daydreaming about a future with him. She felt very self-conscious around him. Months of struggle followed for Lily, as she sought to regain her moorings and keep every thought captive to God.

Teach your daughters to not tease about boys, and how to take teasing about boys. Teasing often results in deep emotional involvement for the unfortunate target, no matter how it may have been intended. Never give your daughter the idea that being single is a disgrace. Encourage her that she can live a happy, fulfilled single life with the Lord as her husband. That is so much better than being unhappily married!

Your daughter will be well equipped for godly womanhood if she has learned to control her thoughts as a youth. Encourage your daughter to maintain a pure thought life, screened by... *Finally, brethren, whatsoever things are true, whatsoever things are honest, whatsoever things are just, whatsoever things are pure, whatsoever things are lovely, whatsoever things are of good report; if there be any virtue, and if there be any praise, think on these things* (Phil. 4:8). A curious mind turned loose will wander into paths that are enticing. Daydreaming and romance stories can be a source of mental sin for girls and feed lust like dry wood feeds a fire. One sister eventually left her devoted husband and five children as a result of daydreaming about a former boyfriend. Protect your dear girl!

Is your daughter aware that there are some males whose first interest is not unselfish love for her, but self-gratification? Does she know that true love will protect purity? A young girl who understands this before she is ready to court has a protection against the advances of the unscrupulous. It also protects her in courtship, even one that starts with high ideals.

A young courting couple, accompanied by their parents, sat with a pastor in his study. Hearts were heavy, and tears kept surfacing. Finally the young man spoke, brokenly confessing that they had fallen into fornication. The young lady confessed also, deep sadness etched in every word. Then her mother spoke, heartbroken. "I have failed in not teaching my daughter what she needed to know before she began courting."

Teach your sons and daughters! Do all you can to spare them the grief and reaping of sin. The fear of God within will be their best protection.

Preparing your daughter for courtship

Let's say your daughter has, by the grace of God, safely made it through the turbulent teen years. Now a godly young man is asking for her friendship. You as parents have taught your daughter purity. Now it is her father's duty and privilege to check out the young man desiring her heart and hand.

Your daughter, now a young lady, has a big part to play in keeping the courtship pure. She needs to, more than ever, dress modestly. She has no idea how much easier modest dress makes life for her boyfriend. If they don't get married, neither one will have those deep regrets if they kept themselves pure. If they do get married, they will have a good foundation for intimacy and have laid a priceless foundation of respect and trust. Purity is the very best gift they can give each other at the altar.

Godly, modest conduct should be a normal part of your daughter's life by now. Encourage her to maintain her thoughts in purity. Temptations are strong when the mind feeds on the forbidden, but if our mind feeds on the good and pure, temptations are minimal. Maintaining a hands-off courtship is vital if they would avoid the snare of immorality. If they don't start touching each other, they are protecting themselves mightily from overpowering temptations. Ask your daughter if her friend has purposed to have a hands-off courtship. If she has any reason to question his moral integrity or if she feels pressured to permit touching to please him, beware! Many girls have slipped into sin by wanting to please their friend.

It may be helpful to discuss with your daughter the four levels of knowing another: practical, spiritual, emotional, and physical. God's design is that they as a couple first communicate on the spiritual and practical level. As trust and confidence grow, emotional ties are formed. This prepares them for a beautiful union of the physical, after marriage. Explain to her how the devil's intent is to twist those totally backwards, first focusing on the emotional and physical. The reaping is marriage to a person you have never learned to know or trust spiritually.

Do not feel intimidated in teaching her high ideals if you have had an impure past yourself. God wants to use that experience to effectively warn your daughter of the pitfalls and reaping, so they can avoid making the same mistakes!

If your youth have fallen sexually, there is forgiveness through the blood of Jesus as they repent, confess, and forsake sin. While they don't need to live under condemnation of past sin, there is a bitter reaping. They will need help from you as their parents and perhaps other mature Christians to help them deal with their past.

Preparing your daughter for marriage

She will do him good and not evil all the days of her life. (Prov. 31:12)
What can you, her mother, do to help your daughter be a wonderful
wife with a proper perspective of intimacy? Her beauty, her whole
body and spirit, will soon be given to her husband. She will find it
the joy of her heart to be totally his, to fully satisfy him intimately,
just as he will seek to fully satisfy her needs (1 Cor. 7).

In your intimate talks, express the joy of marriage, the joy of
giving herself wholly to her husband. A man's way of expressing
love usually includes intimacy. A wife who understands that will
not quickly say, "I am just too tired." A responsive wife who enjoys
intimacy holds an appeal and satisfaction for her husband. The
difference could be compared to a drink from a mud puddle versus a
sparkling glass of cold water on a hot day. Either can meet the need,
but there is really no comparison. A man whose needs are joyfully
met by his wife goes out to face the world as a conqueror. Other
women do not easily entice him; his queen awaits him at home.

The intimate act of marriage is a sacred secret between her and her
husband. If struggles occur, they should make it a matter of prayer as
they together seek God's face. If struggles continue, they should seek
help from godly brethren.

The absolute delight of a marriage in the fear of God cannot be
explained. Witnessing the sparkle on your newlywed daughter's face
as she and her friend join pure hearts and hands is an immense joy
to a mother's heart.

It is worth every effort to share with your daughter from
babyhood on. You will cherish your relationship with her more than
the choicest gold.

*From an article written for the book Siervas del Rey (Servants of the King). Used by
permission of Lamp and Light Publishers.*

Dear Mom & Dad,

I am your child. I am now twenty years old, but at one time I was
only ten. Back then I wished I was twenty; now I sometimes
wish I was ten again so I could do differently the things that are
now set in stone. You do not know this, but when I was about the
age of ten, I started doing many things that you never learned about.

When I was in that stage of hormonal adjustments and beginning
to change physically, I began to have sexual desires. I did not know
what was happening, and I would not have told you—you did not
ask and I was afraid. It was new and different. I remembered years
before, when I was five or six, an older girl had told my siblings and
me about the facts of life. I wondered often about the things she
told us. The same girl asked me to show her my breasts when I was
eleven years old, because she thought I was too young to wear a bra.
In exchange, she showed me her own fully developed form; a picture
that will stay with me always. Did you know that, Mom and Dad?

I don't remember for sure how it all began, but around the same time my twin sister showed me how to do something very bad. I felt guilty, but the guilt was mixed with a taste of pleasure I had never felt before; a thrilling pleasure that helped me escape from the pain of my mother's depression and my father's preoccupation. Lots of times this happened. Sometimes we lay in our own beds and played with only ourselves; other times we played with each other. Always, even as a child, I felt guilty and told God I was sorry after I was finished. I wondered if I would go to hell for doing such unspeakable things.

When we discovered that our best friends from church also did these things, we were not only surprised, but we suddenly felt a closer kinship with them. We spent long hours at their house when we needed babysitting, and talked about many things that children should never talk about. They taught us new things.

Then I did something I look back upon with a very deep sense of shame. One day when I was ten or eleven, you left us children at my cousin's house after school. I taught my cousin some of the same things. I do not know how hard she may have struggled after that, and I have since told her I am sorry, but no apology could recompense for what happened that day! I wish you would have known.

I accepted Christ at a very young age and attempted to lay aside those things of my past. I had grown from a little girl into a budding young woman, and these changes made it even harder to keep myself pure. Though my twin and I no longer masturbated together, very little had changed for us individually.

By the time I gained gradual victory over that chapter of life, a new problem had entered into my life. Remember Joseph, the worker we hired for several years in the woodworking shop? He was like our brother he said, and we accepted him as such. I alone seemed to struggle. Why did I go to bed after a day of sanding furniture with him, unable to sleep? Why did his touches make me shiver, and his tone of voice sometimes make me shrink back in fear? Why did those hugs and kisses (if only you knew how he tricked me into giving that first kiss!) feel *wrong*, somehow? Why couldn't I accept it and love him like the rest of my siblings seemed to?

I didn't know. I didn't understand why I hated myself, and why I hated Joseph. I thought something was wrong with me. The only time I tried to express myself in my journal, I went back and marked it all out again. I didn't understand why I felt so dirty and ugly inside. I didn't understand why, when you mentioned that you didn't like us working such long hours together, you did nothing more about it. Why didn't you see what was happening? Why did you sometimes go to bed when Joseph worked overtime and leave us alone with him? It is only by the grace of God that nothing worse happened; only by the grace of God that he never stole our virginity. It could have happened so, so effortlessly!

Joseph went out of my life, and I was able to receive kind help from caring friends. Thank God for them!

Crushes were something I battled over the years, but one day I realized the young man I had begun to care about was receiving far more affection than a simple crush. "Are you in love with him?" a close friend asked me, and I took my heart to court and knew I was. It was a love that should have been reserved for one man only, and even though he never knew, I gave my love to a man who did not ask for it. The journey back to emotional purity was among the most agonizing I have ever been on. At times I still feel near tears when I remember those days of struggle and crucifixion. I felt dreadfully alone.

I am dating now, and my boyfriend is a wonderful Christian man, far above what I deserve. We had been dating several months when these things came back to trouble me, making me once again feel used and unclean. I felt forgiven by God, but how do I know my boyfriend will forgive me? For the first time, I was struck with the truth that I had not only sinned against God, but also against my own body and my future husband. Suddenly I feared that he would not want to date me if he knew that such things lurked in my past, and I knew I could not hold it against him if he wanted to discontinue our courtship. Satan brought back all the pain and failures of the past and dangled them before me. I did not feel innocent enough to be worthy of a godly man. How bitterly I longed to erase these marks forever from my past! What drastic measures I would take to wipe it all away!

For the sake of protecting our courtship purity, I have said very little to my boyfriend so far. He knows I have regrets. He knows I have not always kept myself pure. He has regrets from his past, too, but I am not the one to tell his story. "Neither do I condemn thee; go, and sin no more," he wrote to me, in response to my troubled letter of confession and regret. I curled up in a ball on my bed and thought I would never stop crying. That I could be forgiven was nearly inconceivable. I felt as though God was giving me a second chance, a new beginning and a clean slate.

God has been faithful, and His forgiveness is full. But there are still scars, still a reaping for those things that should never be spoken of among us. I wish with my whole heart that I could enter marriage innocent of the evil the world holds. I wish valiantly that my heart was still reserved; my body untouched. I wish for a scar-free past! I wish someone had warned me, had cared more, had tried harder to see what was happening. I am left with a burning desire to warn others, to stand in front of a thousand girls and plead with them not to do what I did.

I am writing to you, Dad and Mom, instead. Why didn't you see what was happening? Why didn't you protect our purity, and guard it carefully as the precious gem it is? Why was it okay to make light of sacred things, and why didn't we feel free to come and talk with you about these things? Why didn't you carefully help me protect my heart and body?

The other day I caught my little brother masturbating. He is only a child. How many times have I heard you say that he is "young and innocent"? It breaks my heart.

As God has forgiven me, I forgive you. But I have many little sisters in this world, and my heart longs to reach out and protect them. That is in your place, and your position. Do not think it is a good thing to withhold their education; they will learn by themselves or from the perversion of others. I am confident you do not want that to happen. Do not think that just because you have not heard or seen signs of abuse, they are innocent and pure. That's what you thought about me, and it wasn't true. Please carefully guard who they spend time with. Do their friends have stable, concerned parents? My friends didn't.

Talk to them, and tell them how special and valuable the gift of purity is. Help them understand the awe-inspiring sacredness of the marvelous way man and woman were created, and the importance of doing everything possible to protect that purity. Impress upon them the tremendous beauty of entering marriage completely pure. They will not learn these things on their own.

I write to you, because I am

Your Daughter

Preventing

Sexual Abuse in the Home

Marvin Wengerd

Parents have a great responsibility to protect their innocent children from lifelong scars that come with sexual abuse. Causing an offense to a child has serious consequences before God. Jesus says that *it were better that a millstone were hanged about his neck, and that he were drowned in the depth of the sea* (Matt. 18:6). Sexual abuse is only one way to offend a child, but it is the most horrible way. Parents who are careless with this responsibility are careless at their own peril before God. God's wrath hangs over those who offend the weak and vulnerable of the human family.

1) Develop a spiritual atmosphere in your home. Dads, you are responsible to lead in family devotions. Sing. Pray. Read the Bible. Show your children how big God is. Show them His love for every soul. Show them His hatred for evil. Impress on your family the importance of purity.

2) Have a holy view of intimacy. Holiness and purity in regards to sexual things starts with parents having a holy view of intimacy.

If parents have the concept that intimacy between husband and wife is shameful and naughty, or connect intimacy with shame and guilt, the devil has a highway into your child's life. Sexual things are holy and created by God for procreation and pleasure. Leftover shame and guilt from sinful courtships poison the well and often keep parents from relating to each other and to their children in a holy way. Repent before God, confess sin, and make restitution, then begin developing a holy attitude about sexual things.

When Dad is frustrated with intimacy, or when Mom feels used and unfulfilled in their intimacy, it becomes almost impossible for them to relate in a holy way regarding sexual things to their children. Parents, seek help with these issues. Don't brush them under the carpet. Don't wait for them to go away. Get help.

3) Have high standards for reading material. Do a thorough housecleaning of all your reading material. Newspapers are a constant source of lewd sexual ideology. Many hunting magazines should be canceled. Burn romance books, for they stimulate illicit sexual fantasies and ideas. Call in to have your name taken off of mail-order catalogs. Many catalogs we get today would have been considered pornographic seventy-five years ago. Screen the mail before the children browse through it.

4) Maintain high standards of modesty in the home. Parents should model modesty first. Dad without a shirt or Mom with immodest nightclothes are a good way to create a low view of modesty in the home. Girls should avoid provocative night wear.

Bathing boys and girls together after two years old should be avoided. Most children can retain a memory of happenings at two, especially if the happening was dramatic. Dad should not bathe girls past four years old. Many parents compromise here for the sake of efficiency—too many children, too little time. Run them through together is the thought. Parents should never be naked in front of a child that is older than two. Dad and the boys should not shower as a group. Keeping these boundaries clear helps a child avoid carelessness when he is away from home. If his training has been careless, his life will be careless, too. Respect and clear gender lines are two of the best preventions of abuse.

All bedroom and bathroom arrangements in the home must be carefully evaluated. Have we created situations where abuse is easy? Likely? Do our sleeping arrangements open the door to temptation?

Children get older every day and what may have been okay a year ago may be compromising today.

Parents have a grave responsibility to protect their girls from sexual abuse. If you want to err, err on the side of safety. Don't err on the side of carelessness and neglect.

5) Talk to your child about sexual things. This is often really hard for parents. What age should we start? How much should we say? Should Dad talk to the girls or should Mom?

Before a child begins school he should be taught that sexual things are not for discussion except with parents. He/she should be taught that no one should ever touch or see his/her private parts. This should be done discreetly enough that the child does not feel unnecessarily fearful, but frank enough that he/she has an exact understanding of what is inappropriate. You want a very open relationship with your child in regards to sexual things, so if something should go wrong that they will come to you immediately. Teach them to be suspicious and avoid activity and children that have that "Now don't you tell your parents about this" tone.

When a girl reaches the age of menstruation, Mom should talk to her about that in enough detail so her fears about what's happening are gone.

Dad should talk openly to ten to twelve-year-old boys about masturbation and their awakening sexual awareness. Many parents feel too fearful to talk about these things, only to find out later that they have already been talked to by their peers. When a child learns sexual things from peers, it is almost always in an unsanctified or dirty way. When a child learns that sex is dirty, being secretive about it is their natural response.

Often a child's first exposure to sexual things comes with observing animals. This provides a good opportunity for the parent to explain how God made animals to reproduce and how the cycle of birth works. If parents treat the child's observations with a heavy dose of "don't look; it's naughty" the child's curiosity is stimulated even more, but now his concept of reproduction is poisoned with guilt and shame. In general children should not have excessive exposure to breeding animals, but neither should parents treat it as totally off limits for a child either.

6) Guard who your child is with and where.

A very high percentage (over 80%) of sexual abuse occurs with someone the child knows well and trusts. Brothers, cousins, uncles, and boys in the neighborhood or church. In some cases, even Dad. It's easier to warn our children about strangers, but reality requires that we warn more about those we should be able to trust.

Never allow girls and boys to use the bathroom together. The haymow, dimly lit barns, basements, and upstairs are important places to watch. Going for a pleasant walk in the woods can turn into a nightmare.

Should we rethink what we do with our children during council meeting and communion? Is leaving them alone all day without parental supervision the best we can do? Is it the right thing to do?

When you attend family reunions or other gatherings check on your child. If you perceive that the situation is risky remove them. Speak up. Ask others to do the same. Know what's going on. Sure, you may raise a few eyebrows if you're perceived as overly protective. But God did not entrust the child to the community or to the extended family—God trusted your child to you.

At twelve to fifteen years old begin teaching your child about pure courtship. Teach boys age-appropriate concepts about girls and dating. Teach girls how to keep their hearts for the one God has for her. Talk to them about the sacredness of marriage and how courtship is a preparation time for marriage.

7) Know how sexual abuse looks and blow the whistle.

Here are three stages of sexual abuse. We will start with the mildest form and transition to the most severe.

Exposure.

At this stage children uncover their private parts for other children to see. Children sometimes do it as a group, daring each other by turns. The unwilling one is mocked. Some may say exposure is not exactly abuse. Technically it isn't, but the memory and effects often follow a girl into adulthood. In many cases the shame and guilt it causes have very similar effects as more severe forms of abuse. If a trusted adult exposes himself to a girl, exposure is even more traumatic and harmful. When men scan a woman's body in lust many women express feeling "exposed" and "violated."

Fondling.

In fondling, a girl's genital area, legs, or breasts are touched or stroked. Fondling is a violation of a child's privacy and a weight on her conscience. She often begins viewing her own body with distaste and even hatred. Fondling has serious legal implications.

Fornication, rape, or incest.

When a girl's body is penetrated the Bible calls it fornication. The legal system calls it rape if it occurs between two people who are not family and the girl/woman was forced. Incest is the word that is used when a dad or brother commits fornication with a daughter or sister.

This is the worst form of sexual abuse and often holds lifelong trauma for the victim. God hates it. The law of the land calls it a crime and imprisons men for it. And the church must place herself squarely on the side of God and the law. It is a crime against a holy

God first, against an innocent, vulnerable child second, and against the law of the land third.

The church that is unable or unwilling to denounce this cannot be accurately called a church and deserves the public condemnation it is sure to receive.

In every stage of abuse a parent needs to blow the whistle. Silence guarantees more victims. More victims guarantee even more victims.

In the first two stages every parent whose child was involved needs to know. Every parent whose child could become a victim needs to be warned.

In Stage 3 the parents of both the victim and perpetrator need to know. The ministry of the church needs to know. And finally, even the law needs to know.

Sexual abuse—its ugly fingers reach into the lives of so many now. It must be stopped. It must be stopped because the law is against it, but more importantly a holy God waits to see if we will once again sweep it under the carpet of cultural pride and spiritual indifference or if we will fall on our faces in repentance and cry out to Him for mercy and help.

More Than Cows and

Brenda Nolt

It was a beautiful sunny, Sunday afternoon. We had heard that one of the families from our school had a new baby so, as was traditionally the custom, we decided to pay them a visit. There were also many other families there that afternoon.

As we had expected, the mothers all sat in the kitchen, close by the new mother. They all had their own babies on their laps or playing by their sides, besides the other toddlers playing in the same room. The men all sat in the living room.

The mothers spent a lot of time talking about the new baby. He was a nephew to most of them and his looks were discussed, besides things like sleep habits, diaper rashes, colic, and many other such subjects. The other mothers' babies were discussed too, whether it was their behavior, potty training, eating habits, and so forth. Though the mothers did discuss the person that has cancer, the new couple, and the coming school picnics, the conversations often went back to the babies and toddlers. Most of the school-aged girls and the other mothers fondly took a turn to hold the new baby. Yes, a newborn babe is a very special blessing indeed. If you are a mother to little ones, it is an interesting subject to discuss.

The dads then, what did they talk about? They talked about farming. There is nothing wrong with talking about farming. It is common ground and a way of life for most of them. Here also, there is a wide range of things to discuss. How the cows are milking, what the milk price is, or maybe milk fever, mastitis, Holstein vs. Jersey, grazing vs. traditional, etc. Then they want to talk about field work; whether the manure is all hauled, what kind of corn to plant, tillage vs. no-till, haylage vs. dry hay bales, and so on. Very often, the subject of money is discussed, the cost of new equipment, seed prices, ect. It is an interesting subject to discuss.

So all in all it was a good afternoon, right?

Was it?

What did the parents not know about that afternoon?

Did they know what the older children were doing? The ones that are older than the toddlers that stayed by their mother's side. The mothers would never have considered letting those little children outdoors unsupervised. Why not? They wanted to keep them safe. They did not want them to get lost in the woods, or go out on the road, or go to the pond or creek. So they watched them and kept them safe.

Don't they want to keep their other children safe?

Do they think that since they are old enough to stay out of physical dangers then there are no other dangers out there?

Do they think that from age four or five on up all is innocent play?

Did the parents not know that all those little boys, those about age four to nine, were already learning how to vandalize other people's property? That they were up in the attic of the little summer house and threw everything down that was up there. They did not really mean to make such a big mess, but one of them threw one thing and another one threw another. With so many boys together they got carried away. One of those things was a little kiddie pool that they then used like a trampoline and made large holes into it. They were having so much fun throwing things, in fact, that they broke the glass in one of the windows besides ruining a few other things. When they became tired of that sport they were happy to find the nice big sandbox. They played nicely for a while, but of course there were not enough tractors and scoops for so many little boys. One of them became frustrated and threw a handful of sand into the other one's eyes. When he cried and started heading for the house, the other one called him a momma baby. When that one started his taunting cry, three or four others joined in. The boy with the sand in his eyes then only went to lie under the tree instead of telling his mother like he would have wanted to.

What about the little girls? The girls were playing with the dolls, but there were more girls than dolls. One bigger girl scorned a little girl and told her that because she has such crooked teeth, she is not allowed to help them play. She would not have usually done such a thing, but there was such a big group of girls that day and that one girl was not one of her elite group of cousins. Once one of them scorned her, another noticed her different-looking shoes. So there was another thing to mock her about. This little girl did not go and cry under the tree; she only cried inside and became more insecure and self-conscious of her looks. She kept to the back of the crowd and sadly watched them play.

Please, did the parents know what the older boys were doing?

First they went through the barns and farm equipment. They did not really hurt anything, but were they being respectful of the other people's property when they started the motors, chased the animals, and went through everything? Next they went across the road to the schoolhouse. Here they managed to open a window and climbed inside. They were smart enough to not leave any signs that they were there. They did not want to be questioned, and the youngest of them was sternly admonished not to tattle or he would pay in a way he would not like! But they did go into the children's desks and root through their things. They even went into the girls' bathroom and went through the cabinets there. The parents would be glad to know that they did play some ball in the school yard too.

Did the parents know that one of the boys smuggled a dirty magazine along and showed it to all the other boys? Did they know that into those boys' minds were burned images that would never leave them?

Did the parents know that one of the 13-year-old boys found a partly burned cigarette along the road, and using a smuggled lighter, lighted it and gave it to the other boys to try a puff? Did they know that when one of the boys refused to try it, the others laughed and mocked him, calling him a preacher lover?

<hr />

Is there more to Sunday afternoon visits than cows and babies?

Do parents care more about their children than they do about getting a chance to visit with other parents? Do they care more about their children than they do about their banking accounts and the price of milk? Are there any of these subjects so interesting that they cannot leave the house to check on the welfare of the older children?

Shouldn't all our children be supervised and checked on regularly? Shouldn't all those mothers and fathers care enough about all the rest of their children, besides their babies, that they go and check on them at least several times every afternoon? Even if they were told to respect other people's property, feelings, and wishes, do parents realize that though children can be told all these things, they will get carried away when they are left unsupervised for extended periods of time with groups of other children? Shouldn't they have something constructive to do for all those hours?

Where is the responsibility of the fathers on Sunday afternoons? Does their role go beyond taking care of the animals in the morning, then taking all the children along on a Sunday afternoon visit and forgetting about them until it is time to go home again? Shouldn't they be making sure they are not just wandering around, looking for something to do? Isn't it in the father's place to be telling their sons, about aged 10 and older, that there are evil men that make bad books and magazines? Then also what to do if one of the other boys wants to show them something like that? How important is this in our day and age?

Are the mothers aware what kind of things can happen to their daughters on Sunday afternoons? We still remember vividly one Sunday when everyone was sitting in the house in a setting very similar to the one in this story, only it was a Sunday dinner invitation that day. One of the mothers got up and went to check on the children. Maybe she'd said an extra prayer for the safety of her children that morning that she suddenly had that prompting to go and check. Either way, she found a group of school-aged and younger boys and girls together in the haymow of the barn. Some of them were in various stages of immorality. These little children did not have evil intentions. They were only innocent children playing together for long periods of time unsupervised. If this mother had not intervened this would have turned into a very serious problem. Our oldest son was still a baby at the time, but it made such an impression on us that we never forgot. We noticed that thereafter, whenever the family was together, this mother went to check on her children, not only once but at least several times. Shouldn't all girls be taught the specifics concerning discretion with their clothing and when to come quickly to tell their mother when something happens in this line? Are we as mothers doing all we can to protect our daughters' purity and innocence?

So yes, it was good and right to enjoy such a Sunday afternoon together, sharing the joys and challenges of parenting and farming. But isn't it even more important to know where our children are and what they are doing?

After we came home from visiting this family, we sat and talked with our own children about things that we and they had seen that day, and we were filled with a deep sadness. It really made us wonder; could it be that some of the reason some areas struggle with vandalism, pornography, abuse, disrespect for others, or mocking with their youth is because it started before their children were even in school, on a Sunday afternoon?

Will not God bless us with protection and safety for our children if we are willing to put in this effort?

Therefore shall ye lay up these my words in your heart and in your soul...And ye shall teach them to your children, speaking of them when thou sittest in thine house, and when thou walkest by the way, and when thou liest down, and when thou risest up (Deuteronomy 11: 18-19).

What Would You Do If…?

How to hold a family safety training

Gina Martin

Although I grew up in a sheltered environment, I know we have an enemy who is seeking to destroy our children's purity. As the world becomes more wicked, my children may be confronted with evil in ways I never was as a child. I have given my children brief warnings against sexual predators and temptations when the topic came up. But I worried that I had skipped a child or it was too long between reminders. I tend to procrastinate with difficult topics like these, but I know that the safety of my children is too important to leave to chance.

I hope my children never have to face a situation where their purity is in danger. I don't expect to experience a house fire either, but every year our family has a fire drill to prepare for this unlikely event. I don't want our children to be fearful of fires, but it is important that they know what to do in an emergency. Isn't the safety of my child's moral purity even more important?

I decided to combine our fire drill with teaching about other dangers as well. We kept the tone of this "safety training" light and fun. The children (ages 2-12) were often laughing, but now I am more confident I have taught all of our children what to do in various emergencies. We plan to continue this safety training at least once a year so that the information is reviewed, reinforced, and practiced.

During our safety training, I would ask "What would you do if..." and give a scenario. The children would then do or say whatever was appropriate for that emergency. Here are some ideas in case you want to hold your own safety training.

We began with a fire drill. First we reviewed basic fire safety such as crawling under smoke, stop-drop-and-roll if clothes ignite, and not opening up hot doors. We discussed the best options to escape from each room of the house. Then each of the children went to a different room, and I set off the smoke detector. Each child was to make their way to our designated meeting spot (our woodshed).

Next we reviewed how to call 911. Even children who don't have a phone in their home need to know how to make an emergency call. We practiced dialing the phone (though of course we didn't actually place a 911 call). I then asked the children what they would do if I were hurt. They discussed when they should call 911 and when it would be okay to just call their dad's cell phone for help.

Then we practiced finding a safe spot in case of a bad storm. We talked about lightning storms and tornadoes and safe places to wait out a storm. The children had fun running for the cellar.

Next we talked about appropriate interaction with strangers. I asked the children if they knew what they should do if someone at the park asked them to come see the cute puppies in a truck. I want them to know it is fine to accept candy from a stranger when Mom or Dad is with them but not to go with a stranger when a parent isn't along.

We talked about what to do if someone does something that

makes the child uncomfortable, such as touching their body in private areas, grabbing their arm to force them to come, or anything that feels inappropriate. Our children have been taught to be polite, especially to adults, but we practiced shouting, "Stop! Help!" I told them it is okay to make a scene and be loud, even in a public place, if they are ever in any kind of danger.

I also warned them that sometimes people who want to hurt children look very nice. They may even be someone they know well, such as a neighbor, teacher, or family member. The person might say the activity is not wrong or threaten them with danger if the child tells their parents what was done. Our children know to never keep secrets from their parents (surprises such as birthdays are okay), because a person who threatens a child to keep a secret is afraid of being caught and punished.

No, these are not fun conversations to have with our children. That is why I tried to keep it as lighthearted as possible. I said, "What would you do if someone is doing wrong and they said, 'Don't tell your parents about this or I'll hurt you'?" I want my children to know it is okay to disobey an adult in some conditions. I also want them to know that I'm not afraid or embarrassed to talk about these things so they will not be afraid to talk to me if needed.

Most of all I want my children to know that God is always with them. I have heard countless examples of God's safety when people called on His name. There seems to be power in verbally and audibly calling on Jesus. So we practiced saying, "Jesus, help me." I want my children to know that even if I am not with them, they have a far more powerful Friend who is always available.

Last we talked about temptations. We discussed the various ways we can harm our body. I asked what they would do if a friend offered them cigarettes, drugs, or alcohol. They shouted, "My body belongs to Jesus and I can't do that." We also talked about the need to protect our eyes, ears, and mind. We discussed the difficulty of forgetting something that is seen or heard. I warned against ungodly music and evil pictures that may be on a friend's phone or magazine. Again it is both a comfort and a warning that God is with us and can see what we do and help us stand against temptations. As our children become teens, I can add advice on appropriate interactions between young men and women and the importance of keeping relationships pure.

Our safety training took less than an hour and I think my children would describe it as fun. Like most parents, I hate to introduce the thought to our children that some people could harm them. But just as we warn against playing with matches, we need to warn our children against the greater dangers that could burn their souls.

Safety training does not seem to prompt fear in my children, but if your children become fearful, demonstrate calling on God by praying often with your child. I remember when my brother asked my mom to pray every night that we would not have a house fire. My mom did not brush off his request, but prayed especially for him and his fears every night. Today my brother is a confident, well-adjusted man with his own children.

God is with our children. And God is with our children's parents as we do our best to wisely guide, warn, and protect them on their journey to adulthood. ❀

Consequence
AND
Change
Lena Martin

With the Lord there is mercy, and with Him is abundant redemption. Psalm.130:7

PHASE 1—A GIRL IN CONFUSION BECAUSE OF HER LIFESTYLE

It was my first day with the youth group. Making new friends stood invitingly before me. There was one woman in particular, four years older than myself, who was very outgoing, and popular in the crowd. This woman singled me out and began showing an interest in me. This was comforting to me, as I was shy and awkward by nature, especially in such a large group. The next weekend, and the next, this woman sought me out, making mention of how special it was to have me for a friend. The woman told me of the hard times in her childhood. Her father was frequently absent from home, and then passed away while she was young. Her stories filled my heart with compassion and a desire to comfort her. A few similar weekends followed with more stories of hardship.

This woman invited me to her house one Saturday night. I accepted a ride in her car. While we were sitting on her sofa, she again sought my sympathy. She gave me a hug and then suddenly began fondling my breasts. I was startled! I had mixed feelings and new sensations that stirred and excited me. The woman then invited me to the bedroom.

After a few weekends of the same, this perpetrator asked, "Do you know what you call what we are doing?"

"No," I retorted.

"It's called homosexuality," she responded.

A few weeks later, I was thinking of this secret life I was living and asked this woman, "Should we go someplace and find help to stop doing this?"

In response she said nothing, only stared ahead with glazed eyes.

Girls who choose the lesbian lifestyle are taking on a continuous lonely life. The girl who has consented to be homosexual is in the grips of sinful passion that traps her mind in unresolved longings. Development of relationship skills is greatly hindered and character destroyed. The fulfillment she looks for never comes, because Jesus is fullness, and only He fills the longings of the heart.

Some days my confusion intensifies so that it takes great effort to think and function. The empty feeling I have, as constant as the air I breathe, drags me into isolated canyons of my mind, away from the friends I once enjoyed. I put on a smile, and on occasion when talking with others I think, "What is wrong with me? I wish I could be real."

Unto the pure all things are pure; but unto them that are defiled and unbelieving is nothing pure (Titus 1:15). Even a friendship card can be given with a sinful fantasy in mind.

Was God with me? I believe the times I felt really empty were the times God was drawing me to Himself. I surfaced to consider truth, but I didn't know where He was. When I found heart change, I remembered gasping a prayer, eyes blind and hollow, "Show me, God, where you are."

I hate this double life I am living. Yet, I seek it out again, accepting plans for another weekend with her. At the same time my sinful life crushes peace and hope in me. Around others I fake being normal, my self-worth diminishing. I ask myself, "Will this always be my life; the free world out there, and me locked up in ghostly quietness?"

In church one Sunday, the pastor told this biblical parable of a man who planted a fig tree in his vineyard and it gave no fruit. Then he said to the dresser of the vineyard, "Behold, these three years I come seeking fruit on this fig tree and find none: cut it down; why cumbereth it the ground?"

But the dresser of the vineyard answered him, "Lord, let it alone this year also, till I shall dig about it, and dung it: And if it bear fruit, well: and if not, then after that thou shalt cut it down" (Luke 13:6-9).

At that time I was three years enslaved to this sinful lifestyle. "Am I the tree, reserved to one more year?" Later when I had found heart change, I remembered, and knew God was near me that Sunday morning.

One December the youth went Christmas caroling. The night was cold, the truck moved from house to house. I helped sing out the good news that Christ has come to bring hope to a world lost in the darkness of sin. One song spoke through the stillness of my soul, "And though the wrong is oft so strong, God is the ruler yet." Thoughts within had me looking into space; wrong is strong, but where is God?

Still continuing this detestable lifestyle, I felt unable to change the existing habit. One evening I was at youth song practice, and in closing, the leaders of the music class sang a duet, "Shall I crucify my Savior, when for me He bore such loss? Once, oh once I crucified Him; shall I crucify again?" My thoughts accused, "That's me; that's what I am doing."

I could not change my sinful heart, nor quit the practice of seeing my soul mate on weekends, going on now for four years. It was sickening. Pressed down by reckoning with the truth of my need, I set out to find the answer. "I know God is out there somewhere."

oooooooooooooooooooooooooooooooooooooooooooooooooooooooooooooooooooooo

Phase 2—Freedom Sought for and Found

Yes, I had heard the gospel story many times. I had a praying mother, and Bible stories planted faith from my childhood. Sin also played its part in my fallen nature. I wanted to see God big. I read every book in the Danny Orlis series I could lay my hands on. Danny always turned to Christ and found His help in any given difficulty. I also enjoyed reading romance novels by Grace Livingston Hill. These were passed around by friends in my early teen years.

In adolescence I was probably like most girls, facing an unsure future. Being a deep-thinking girl, I dreamed of being a woman of character; my self-focused heart mingled with both good intentions and pride. At fifteen and sixteen there were good friends who shared the "should do's," and the "should not do's" for young people. They were great friends; later they would become my sisters-in-law.

But Satan had lured me off to build with sticks, on a foundation of sand. Without Christ in focus, my self-life took on scheming importance. My hope of developing into some great Christian lady was hanging by a thin string.

Now empty and gasping from the depths of hopelessness, I sought filling, but filling of what, I don't know.

"Revival meetings are going on," said one friend of former years. "I hear they are really good. Would you want to go with me one evening?"

"Yes, I would like to go with you," I said, but my shy nature had me trembling at the thought.

"There is something to have outside of myself, because I see happy people," I mused. The evening had been a good one. The message turned on a light; it was just a speck, but I would not lose it. Jesus died on the cross for my sins. He could change my heart of sin and put a new heart in its place. Repentance and confession of sin by believing, I can become a child of God.

I went home that night; there was light at the end of a dark tunnel. I knelt by my bed and said a simple prayer, "Lord, my sin is heavy, and my life is so dark. You are the light I long for. Take this sin away; wash me clean; come into my heart and make me a new creation; in Jesus' name, Amen."

This new life was joyfully mine, but also seemed strange. Then I remembered, Jesus said, *"Whosoever drinketh of the water that I shall give him shall never thirst, but the water that I shall give him shall be in him a well of water springing up into eternal life"* (John 4:14). I had something better than life; Jesus was my personal Savior. I would take nothing in place of the new joy in my heart. "It is worth the loss of all things." I wanted to tell the whole world, but instead I chose not to tell my story, except for a few words to a few people. But to everyone my joy was evident.

∞∞

PHASE 3—GOD NEVER TURNS HIS BACK; HE NEVER GIVES UP

It had been three years since my conversion; nearly two of those years I volunteered helping handicapped children. One day a letter came from a kind gentleman friend wanting to visit me at Faith

Mission Home where I was staying. We had known each other a long time, but for the first time we shared an interest in sharing a life together. Many came to bless our wedding day, and God blessed our marriage.

In the years that followed I became aware that there is something that still binds me. It was something more than being timid, but I couldn't define it. There was conflict in my heart, and sadly my husband and children felt the conflict. I knew some freedom, but in many ways I remained bound. For too many years I went on trying to hide it, and performed the best I could. Then, with the help of my family, I opened up to tell my story. It was through sharing and prayer that God became my Abba Father. This was the beginning of my journey toward healing. Severe testing took place; my wounded heart was searching for healing, but there was so much pain. There were many times I reacted wrongly. God wanted my heart.

I had come this far by faith, with fear and many strenuous tests. I've faced some of the darkest days in my life. But I know the power of God called me from the brink of destruction, and changed my sinful desires into a desire to please Him. This was a sure sign that God was for me.

Author of "A Trampled Flower Can Rise Again", and the revised edition, *"Trampled Flower"*

AMY'S DILEMMA

Anonymous

Amy's story is not sexual; her story is for all women who encounter abuse in their homes, and for the rest of us.

"Is it ever right for a wife to go for help for her marriage or family without her husband's permission?" Amy was questioning her own long-held beliefs.

"I wouldn't," the bishop's wife answered.

"Have you considered this to its logical end?" Amy pressed her question further, saying, "Please understand, this isn't happening in our home—but if you knew your husband was sexually molesting your daughter and he demanded that you keep quiet about it, would you go for help?"

The bishop's wife thought awhile, then answered slowly, "I don't know. That would be really serious. I think I would."

After further thought, the bishop's wife added, "And I *might* go for help for my marriage, but only if I was sure it was going to end otherwise."

Like the bishop's wife, Amy had long believed that God asked a woman to obey her husband completely. Did not the Bible say a wife was to submit to her husband as to the Lord? Lately, however, she had begun to suspect that she had misunderstood her responsibility before God. If only it were so simple as the stories made it sound: pray earnestly, support him, and keep in God's order; he'll come around.

Amy had loved and prayed for her husband. When Aaron had slammed the door in her face and hissed at her to stay out, she had stayed out; but now she wondered whether Christ would have merely stood outside the study door, praying (and weeping), while a helpless child was penned inside with an enraged and violent father. The law of the land said this made her an accomplice to the abuse. Did the law of God agree?

It hadn't happened every day—not even every week. Aaron usually apologized to her and the children after he lost his temper. She had always forgiven him. With innocent tenderness, the children felt sorry for Daddy when he was so sorry; they readily forgave. Aaron didn't seem aware of all the ways he criticized and belittled her and the children with his words, but they forgave that, too. Privately, Amy explained to the children that Daddy didn't want to treat them like that, but his daddy hadn't spoken lovingly to him, and so he didn't really know how a daddy should talk to his children. She assured them that Daddy loved them and didn't know how badly his words hurt.

Sometimes she tried to talk to Aaron about his injustice. It did little good. She read and reread the Scripture that said a wife might win her husband "without a word." Should she be trying to get him to see what he was doing? Surely she shouldn't tell someone else. Wasn't it in her place to support her husband, and his job to seek help if he wanted it?

More and more, though, Amy wondered how to reconcile this approach with other Scriptures. God commanded His people to take up the cause of the oppressed. He said to care for and protect the weak and the young. Who would care for her children if she didn't? No one else even knew what was happening.

In Matthew 18, Amy read Jesus' instructions that if a brother sins against you, you should go to him alone. If he doesn't hear you, you should take a witness with you. If he still doesn't hear, you should take it to the church. Wasn't Aaron her brother as well as her husband? If she kept quiet, who would help him?

Aaron's physical abuse had ended as the children grew older, but the verbal and emotional abuse continued.

Amy thought back to her conversation with Aaron a few months earlier. "Sam has a cell phone now," she had begun. "I understand he needs it for his job. Could we put some guidelines in place for his protection?"

"We can't discuss anything without arguing," Aaron had said.

"I think we agree on this, Aaron. Both of us want our children to be faithful. Both of us care about their souls. Can we see if we can come together on this?"

"No, unless we have a third party present, we'll just argue. You won't agree with anything I say. It all has to be your way."

"Then could we get a third party to listen as we try to work through this?" Amy asked. "Maybe they can tell us where we are going wrong in our communication."

"No one would be able to understand what is going on if they only listen to one conversation," said Aaron. "The problem is so much bigger than that. No, there is no point in bothering someone else."

In a moment of clarity she herself hardly understood, Amy spoke gently but firmly. "Aaron, if you don't get a third party to help us, I will. I have sought all my life to be the supportive wife God wants me to be, but you have told me for years that I am unwilling to submit to you. I have longed and asked for your leadership, yet you continue to insist that I won't let you lead. You say I am arguing whenever I see anything differently from you.

"Aaron, our children need direction, yet their needs go unresolved year after year, because you say I am so blind to my failings that we'll never resolve things without a third party. It is time to find that third party. If you have not found someone we can trust within a few weeks, I will find someone myself."

Amy had never stood up to Aaron like this; she was surprised at the confidence and peace she felt.

"Just remember," Aaron said ominously, "if you do that without my blessing, it will not turn out well."

Amy had sought out the bishop's wife for advice in her new resolve to find help for them. She had hoped the bishop and his wife could serve as third parties to help her and Aaron, but now she didn't feel safe with that. Nothing so horrible as sexual abuse was going on in their home and they certainly weren't considering divorce. Amy feared she would be considered insubmissive and out of order if she told them her concerns without Aaron's permission.

As Amy prayed and continued her search for a safe place to find help, she began to write down abusive conversations and incidents as they happened. Aaron was so gentle and pleasant in public, and so humble with the church leaders, it seemed unlikely anyone would understand it without seeing clear examples of what was happening.

Amy explained to Aaron that she was writing down some incidents and urged him to do so, too, so that if they ever found a counselor to help them, that counselor would not hear only her side of the story. Aaron refused to write anything down and told Amy she was wrong to do it. "The Bible says love doesn't keep a record of wrongs," he said.

Many times Amy almost destroyed the things she had written

because she was worried that Aaron might be right. Yet when she examined her heart, she knew without a doubt that she was not writing them down to hold them against Aaron, but to bring them to light for the healing of their family.

Amy's writings proved helpful when she and Aaron finally found a minister and his wife who were willing to listen respectfully to both of them. Though she and Aaron had different perspectives of what was wrong in their home, this godly couple was able to understand. They stayed involved with Aaron and Amy's family for a couple of years, ministering healing to Amy and her children and lovingly calling Aaron to accountability for his selfishness and emotional manipulation.

They admonished Amy, explaining that she had wronged her husband by covering for him. She remembered the few times over the years that she had tried to get someone else to understand and reach out to Aaron. Either they didn't know what to do, or else they couldn't understand her reserved and respectful references to the needs in her home. "Oh, God, I so wanted to do right. Did I instead harm my husband as well as my children?" Amy wept as she repented.

ooooooooooooooooooooooooooooooooooooooooooooooooooooooooooooooooooo

The story above is true, and Amy is not alone.

To all the Amys who read this—if you see a persistent pattern of destructive behavior in your husband, appeal to him and pray for him. If that does not resolve it, encourage him to seek help. If he is unwilling, cry out to God to show you a safe place to share your story. Do not let pride or fear drive you to hide what is happening. For the love of both the abused and the abuser, seek help. Do not depend on your submission to heal an abuser.

Brothers and sisters, for Jesus' sake, provide safe places for hurting women and children. Do not assume you will be able to recognize an Amy by her sad and repressed appearance; she may well appear to be a confident, capable, and smiling woman. If we seek to discredit her, blame her for her husband's sin, or in any other way make it unsafe for her to ask for help, God will hold us responsible for the continuing damage and harm to Amy and her children.

To a Child at Night
A.E.M.

Why are you so restless, darling child?
Why the arms that wave about
Though your eyes are closed in sleep?
Let your mama's arms enfold you,
Let her rock and soothe and hold you—
Rest more deeply.

Why art thou so restless, O my soul?
Why the thoughts that churn in doubt
Though thine eyes are closed in prayer?
Let thy Maker's will enfold thee,
Nothing good will He withhold thee—
Trust completely.

As a Roaring Lion

A Concerned Mother

I never would have thought that an action so innocent could wind up taking such a disturbing turn…

As Christians we do our very best to keep the "world" and its evil vices out of our lives. As Christian parents, we do as much as possible to keep evil from our homes, from stealing the innocence of our children, and our own integrity. We go to great lengths to try to keep our home a safe haven.

At least that's what we desire to do.

Satan has other plans. We were struck with that reality in our home.

A woman from Baltimore called to inquire about a puppy we had for sale. Showing great interest, she made plans to come to our home to look at the puppies and place a deposit on one if she liked them.

Two days later she arrived. Although she climbed out of a ritzy-looking car, I was a little taken aback by her appearance.

She sounded different on the phone than she appeared in person. Extremely thin with black and blue spots on her arms, she didn't look healthy. Was she a drug user? She mentioned living in a renovated warehouse, being an artist, and working in a bar. My suspicions deepened. She walked with me into the house to meet the puppies cuddled on our sofa, sound asleep from their recent bath.

I always pray that our home can be a safe haven for those who enter as well, and so I hoped that somehow our life would intrigue her. That she would witness Christ in our life and somehow be encouraged to seek Him. She was respectful, kind, and clean with her speech. Our puppies seemed to please her.

She told me how she had to sell her other dog because he had bitten a child. Grabbing her phone from her pocket, she said, "Here, I'll show you a picture." Still on her knees, pup in hand, she began flipping through her pictures.

She showed me a picture of a cute little dog and we talked about his merits for a while. I never saw my little son standing in the background behind her while she was searching through the phone for the dog picture...

She placed a deposit on the dog and left. We busied ourselves, getting ready to return the pups to their mommy. My husband, who had vacated to the back room, reappeared and I told him my reservations about her lifestyle. It was then that my son dropped his little bomb.

"Mommy, I was standing behind her looking at her pictures when she was flipping through them on her phone, and you know what? There was a picture of someone with no clothes on!" His eyes were big, nose wrinkling in consternation.

Uggh... My stomach did a flip. I think I said something like, "Oh, yuck!" before I could keep my lips shut.

Something so innocent, like the sale of a puppy, now seemed

vulgar.

To be honest, I can't exactly remember what all we said to our six-year-old son. We talked to him about being polite and not looking at other people's phones unless asked to do so. Our older children were shocked, wondering why anyone would ever want to take a picture like that. It was a good opportunity for an important discussion.

My husband and I talked later about how we can keep that from happening again. It was so innocent and yet happened so quickly. Both of us felt that somehow we had failed our son. Failed to protect our children from the vulgar depths of the world. In our own home.

It was only a brief glance. But that was all it took. Even though our son was only six, he registered that picture with great surprise. After something is seen with the eyes, it cannot be unseen.

I feel angry at the evil that is all around us. With God's help we can be victorious, but as we were made aware that day, Satan will do his best to tear down our homes and our families. It makes me tremble at the thought of raising a family in a world so permeated with evil. I thought of the words in 1 Peter 5:8 *Be sober, be vigilant; because your adversary the devil, as a roaring lion, walketh about, seeking whom he may devour.* Isn't that the truth?

Pornography is so prevalent in our world. As Christians we set standards to protect us and our children, but there are so many ways that it can reach into our lives. It makes us, as women, fearful for our sons, our husbands, and our brothers. Fearful of what might happen to our daughters and sons in a society so warped by sin. Not only fearful, but mistrusting. How can I help my husband? My sons? My brothers?

Where will Satan stop? Sad to say, he will stop at nothing. A picture slips in here, a dirty story there…A wrong touch, a lustful desire…Thoughts turn to actions, and actions can cause life-damaging pain. I can find myself becoming almost overwrought with the thought that there is no escape. How can we as parents protect our families? Ourselves even?

First of all, we need to know where to turn. What do we do when we have seen evil? Where do we go for healing? We need to speak to our children about what to do when they are confronted with things like this. In today's world, it is nearly a guarantee that they will be faced with pornography. Simply walking into stores during the summer months can be enough to make a parent cringe and want to cover their eyes. We need to be open like never before. And we need to be honest enough with ourselves to seek forgiveness where we may have failed.

We prayed that our son would be able to forget the picture he had seen. We also thanked him for telling us right away and not trying to hide it or telling his siblings about it in our absence. Children cannot handle the weight of pornography or sexual abuse on their own. They need help to know what to do with the "yuck" that they feel after being exposed to these things.

We do our children a great injustice if we do not talk to them about these things. It is much better to be prepared than to be caught unawares. Talk to your children. In a matter of fact way tell them about these things. You don't have to be graphic or explicit. Just simply explaining to them that there are people who allow Satan to use them to spread evil pictures involving nakedness is enough. It will be so much easier for our children if they feel comfortable talking to us and know that we are aware of these things. It will take away the shock, because they will know that Daddy and Mommy do know that this "stuff" exists and have prepared them for it. Those prepared are usually spared.

Explaining that although we sometimes may not be able to help what we have seen, we can help how often we think about it. We need to seek God's help and take those pictures to Him. "We cannot control the birds that fly over our head, but we can control that none of them makes a nest in our hair." As with any negative thought, we need to recognize its wrongness and take it to the Lord. He alone can cleanse us and make us free.

The same with the possibility of them being abused or misused in a lustful way. It is better to make them aware that, sadly, this evil does exist. Again, you don't need to tell them a graphic horror story for it to sink in. Just a simple explanation of what they must do if they are ever faced with these things or if anyone ever asks them to do something of this nature; *they must tell right away.*

I don't think we can ever stress enough that they need to tell. They need to know that you love them, and you want to know *so that you can protect them.* If they feel bad and feel like you may punish them for this they will keep it a secret. That secret will affect them in negative ways throughout their lives. There is freedom for the child in releasing that evil to an adult who will care enough to protect them.

We have used the example of "dirt or mud" when explaining this to our children. If they have mud up to their shoulders but just wash their hands, are they clean? Of course not! They may need help from their parents to reach the places they cannot clean on their own. These things (pornography and sexual abuse) are like mud that can only be washed away with the help of an adult. When they tell their parents, they can give them the help they may need to get rid of the "dirt." As parents, we can take them to the Lord.

When I think of a topic of this nature, I can quickly become overwhelmed and disgusted with this world... My thoughts often run along the lines of, "Even so, come, Lord Jesus." As a parent, it's so hard to always be on top of things and aware of what things our children are facing. I am so thankful for biblical teachings on purity and a husband who desires his home to be pure.

How can we as mothers help our husbands maintain a pure home atmosphere? Most of all, by being aware. We need to be aware of where our children are and what they are playing and discussing. Proverbs 29:15 says, *The rod and reproof give wisdom: but a child left to himself bringeth his mother to shame.* That gives me clear direction on what I must do. I must be conscious of my children's habits and behaviors, because too much time left by themselves will be their downfall. I must teach modesty to both my sons and daughters and be very diligent in keeping after them. Greatest of all, I must pray faithfully for my husband and my children.

My greatest comfort comes from Jesus and one of my favorite verses is in Psalm 121: *I will lift up mine eyes unto the hills, from whence cometh my help. My help cometh from the Lord, which made heaven and earth.*

He is our Helper. He is aware of the evil in this world. And in confidence we can claim verse seven of Psalm 121: *The Lord shall preserve thee from all evil: he shall preserve thy soul.*

Only in His strength can we stand strong against the roaring lion of this world.

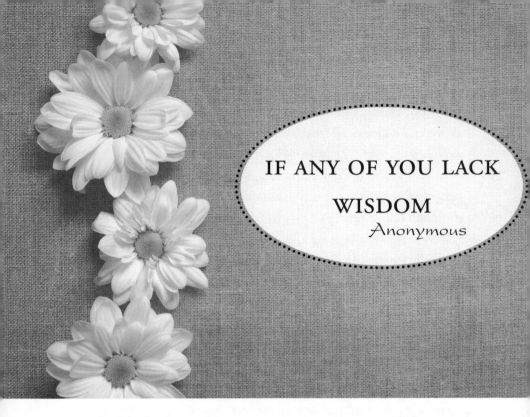

IF ANY OF YOU LACK WISDOM

Anonymous

Are you perplexed about a situation in your home? Do you feel you lack the wisdom to proceed? Pray earnestly; God promises you wisdom.

I didn't want to be suspicious of James, our fourteen-year-old adopted son, but I couldn't shake a feeling of uneasiness when he interacted with the little boys. Though James was always respectful and obedient around my husband and me, our older sons reported conversations and interactions with James that didn't fit with what we saw. Nothing sexual—just a lot of challenges about what our family believed and practiced. Then one time James was caught in a major deception that seemed calculated to seek attention.

Although this event showed us that James was deeply troubled, we still saw no sign of any sexual misconduct—except for the time I opened a door to see him quickly pull his hand out of the front of two-year-old Harry's pants. When I asked James what he was doing, he said he was checking to see if Harry's diaper was wet. It was believable, but I felt uneasy. I kept my eyes wide open.

One rainy day, James asked if he could take the little ones to the barn to play. There were four of them: Jed was nearly James's age but was mentally handicapped, with the mind of a small child; Silas was five, Harry was four, and Chris was only two. James dearly loved children, and it didn't seem fair to say no. I said he could go if he took them all. Surely with four children to potentially tattle on him, James wouldn't try anything unwholesome.

The children came back in a couple of hours, and James chattered happily about all the fun they had and the things they had done. Everything seemed aboveboard.

I had no real reason to mistrust James. Yet our little boys did not seem quite innocent and at peace. Silas seemed sexually curious to an unhealthy degree. Harry seemed troubled and pensive. The little ones seemed somehow different from their well-adjusted older brothers.

I shared my concerns with my husband, and we both began asking God to show us what to do and to deliver our sons from any evil influence in their lives. I clung to our Father's promise to give wisdom to those who ask.

Then we learned that the five-year-old daughter of our acquaintances, the Schmidts, had been molested since babyhood by an older adoptive brother. We had known the perpetrator as a pleasant, gentle boy, a great favorite with those who knew him. James had always reminded me of that boy—smiley, obedient, helpful, and charming.

I called a trusted friend, a close relative of the Schmidts. I wanted to know what had alerted them that something was wrong. I told this friend my uneasiness about James's odd behavior. She advised me to ask the little ones and ask them soon.

We were preparing for a family trip, and I didn't want to wait until we got home. I prayed hard; I had no idea how to do this. I felt I probably had only one chance to get my little boys to open up to me. If James had threatened them, or if they didn't feel safe telling me for some reason, they might lie—and then they might feel they had to maintain that lie. How I needed God's wisdom!

A plan began to unfold to me. I had to give the little boys baths in preparation for the trip. Bath time would be a safe environment where it would be natural to discuss their bodies.

I undressed Silas, crying out to God for the right words and for an open heart in my little boy. When he was in the tub, I said, "Silas, I need to ask you something. It is very, very important that you tell me the truth. And no matter what you tell me, I won't spank you or punish you in any way. It is completely safe to tell me the truth about this, and it is very important."

Silas was a happy little guy who didn't like to think too deeply about things. "Silas, do you promise to tell me the truth completely, no matter what?"

Silas nodded.

"Silas," I said, as I began to wash his private parts, "has anyone ever tried to look at you down here, or has anyone ever touched you here?"

"James does," Silas chirped, "and he lets me touch him, too."

My heart sank, but God gave me grace to continue calmly. I asked him when it had happened, and he mentioned several times, including the rainy day in the barn. All were times when James was with all four of the little ones. I asked if James had touched any of the others; Silas said he had.

"Now, Silas, I need to ask you—has anyone else ever tried to look at you or touch you there?"

He shook his head.

"Are you sure, Silas? Has Andrew ever touched you?"

"No."

I named several of his brothers and boys from church. To each name, he resolutely answered, "No."

I told him I was sorry James had done that to him, and that it had been very wrong of James. That part of his body was a very special place that no one should touch or see, except Daddy or Mama when they were caring for him. I warned him never to do to any other child what James had done to him. I praised him for telling me the truth. I urged him to tell me right away if it ever happened again.

I dried him, dressed him, and turned him loose.

A few minutes later, Harry was in the tub. I asked him the same question I had asked Silas. Harry's little eyes looked sad. "James did," he said. He wrinkled his button nose in disgust. "I didn't like it."

Then it was Jed's turn. Each of his answers perfectly agreed with Silas's and Harry's answers. Last of all I asked Chris. I made my questions very simple this time. He was so little. I asked him if James had ever touched him there. (Silas and Harry had already told me James had touched Chris.) "Yes," Chris answered. When I asked about his other brothers, as a sort of truth check, Chris solemnly said "yes" to every question. I decided a two-year-old's word does not constitute reliable testimony.

Though my heart felt sick as I dressed Chris, I was filled with rejoicing and praise to God for revealing this now, rather than several years later.

After the trip, my husband confronted James, who readily and tearfully confessed to everything the little boys had said.

Home was not the same after that. Not wanting to single out James, we didn't let the little boys go outside alone with any of the older brothers, but that seemed impractical, abnormal, and unfair. Finally we explained to James that while we would not be limiting the other boys' time together, we would not be letting him care for the little ones until he had been faithful for a long time. He seemed to understand, but many years later he told me this decision had made him feel angry and bitter.

The watchfulness required in a situation like this is very trying. A home is designed to operate on trust, and that trust was gone. I cringed whenever James lifted the little ones into their chairs at mealtimes or buttoned their jackets. He had a way with children, and they adored him. I could never relax.

We may never know if we did the right thing, but after asking counsel of our pastor and another trusted brother in the church, we found another home for James in a nearby state. It was a strong, loving home, with a few young people just older than James, but no little ones.

For a few months James seemed to do well, then he grew sullen and angry at being away from home. Soon he initiated inappropriate conduct with a couple of other boys. His foster parents remained patient and encouraging, but eventually James demanded to be brought home. They brought him home, and an older couple in our home church took him in.

From there James spiraled downward. Today he is using drugs, wearing a dress and makeup, and calling himself Angela.

And the little boys? After those memorable baths, they returned to happy, transparent little boys again. A year or so later, when they were tucked into bed at night, someone mentioned what James had done, and Harry's worried little voice asked, "James told us not to tell you, but did I tell you?" Clearly, he didn't remember the evening in the bathtub.

"Yes, Harry, you told me, but you did the right thing. No one should ever tell you not to tell your mama something. You were a very good boy to tell me what happened."

We discussed it some more in that safe and peaceful place, and they seemed satisfied.

I worried about the long-term effects in the little boys' lives. Would the violated become violators? Eventually we asked the leadership from our church to come and pray with us over our little boys, that God would break any strongholds Satan may try to hold in their lives as a result of this. We prayed for full deliverance in the name of Jesus.

After that I had peace.

Today those little boys are men—pure men, men of integrity. We have discussed these things openly, and they are free. God heard my cry for wisdom all those years ago, and He kept his promise.

Never ignore red flags or feelings of uneasiness. Ask counsel of experienced parents. Pray for wisdom. God is counting on you to protect those little ones, and He will give you what you need.

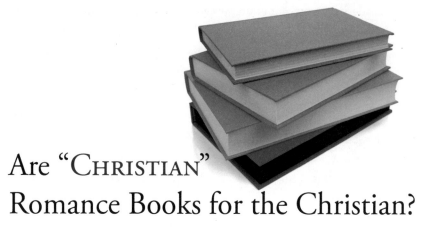

Are "CHRISTIAN" Romance Books for the Christian?

Anonymous

Reading material is often the gateway to impurity. If we want to end abuse we must take an honest look at our books.

Where do I begin on this topic that I feel so passionate about?! For starters, I never even heard of "inspirational fiction" until after I began on the Christian way. Somewhere along the line, I was introduced to "Christian" romance books. And I loved them! It started out pretty mild, as most things do. But over time, I moved from one author to the next. A brother in faith brought this to my attention, along with the Holy Spirit convicting me of my sin and addiction to these books. "Sin? Addiction?" you might say. Yes, sin and addiction. I can only speak for myself, but I feel that romance books affect a woman the same way that pornography affects a man.

"Oh, but *my* romance books aren't that bad," you might say. Let me ask you this: Would you mind showing *any* line in the book to your minister? I've seen sisters with books in their possession that I once read. I remember the stories well. I would blush to tell you what some of them are about. And yet, it's all under the name of "Christian" fiction. Are all Christian romance books sinful?

Obviously, some are much worse than others, but it's hard to know what it's going to be like sometimes until you start reading it.

The Amish-looking ones aren't any better. I often wondered what the Amish would think if they ever read one…these books are not written by Amish authors and often give a false view of the Amish people. Often the main character becomes more modern and pursues an "English" man, all of which the author makes seem to be right. I was not raised in an Amish or Mennonite community, but I have enough respect for them that I don't think they'd appreciate this!

I gave up romance books just a few months before I received my marriage proposal from my husband. I do not believe this was a coincidence. My husband personally thanked the brother who wrote to me of his concern, as he was thankful I was not bringing these books into our marriage with me.

I did a Bible study several years later, regarding books in general. I am including the whole thing, as I've come across many sisters who read these books. It is confusing to the world (the librarians know what books we read…just ask them!). There is something wrong with this picture! Do we take comfort in the fact that we look "right" even though we are participating in things, often in secret, that are contrary to God's Word? This is the type of thing that Jesus was getting at when He spoke of the scribes and Pharisees. And I, during this time of my life where I read romance books, was one of them!

I hope that what follows will benefit those who struggle with a romance book addiction. Please do not assume that I think every fiction book out there is terrible. Not at all! I love to read (although now I stick with nonfiction). But I know there are sisters out there who are struggling with romance books just like I did, to the degree that I struggled. This article is written for you.

ROMANCE BOOKS

Reading is an enjoyable pastime for many people. What we read often influences us in a negative or a positive way. Romance novels are a particular concern for many reasons. Yet they appeal to many women, including some sisters in our faith. This could be resulting from books they have read in their unconverted life and has been carried over into their adult lives. Some single members read romance novels out of curiosity of what married life is like. Others read romance novels in search for emotional satisfaction in life. This article is referring to fiction novels, specifically (but not limited to) romance novels. *Prove all things; hold fast that which is good* (1 Thess. 5:21).

What are the concerns?

1. Romance novels usually portray an inaccurate picture of married life, harmful for both a married and a single person. The story line is written with the intent to keep the attention of the reader, and is often not based on reality. For a single person, romance novels will often make a sister struggle with her single status. For the single sister, "thy Maker is thy husband." I, who once struggled to overcome the temptation to read romance books, read them to compensate for what I thought I was missing as a single person. But when we are "in love" with Christ, we will feel satisfied and content in whatever state we are in.

The way the characters in most romance novels find a helpmate is rarely in agreement with our practice of marriage by faith. This inconsistency can lead to discontentment regarding our way of finding our life's companion. For the married sister, she may be tempted to neglect her husband, children, or household duties as the story consumes her thoughts and steals away her time. She may, with or without realizing it, compare her marriage to the one portrayed in the story, and become dissatisfied with things in her own life. How many female characters in modern fiction books will inspire women to be sober, chaste, keepers at home, etc. (Titus 2:4-5)? How often is physical beauty emphasized more than inner beauty (Proverbs 31:10-31)?

In addition, if it's not right for the single sister, should a married sister take this liberty and risk offending a weaker sister?

2. There are different types of romance books, some mild and some very sinful. Do not console yourself in the fact that you could be reading something "much worse." You could be reading something "much better," if that's the case...God's Word.

Libraries often have a sticker on Christian romance books that says "Christian." However, they may contradict biblical principles. The characters do not always behave in a Christ-like way. Many so-called Christian romance books are not only appealing to the emotions, but also contain some form of sexual appeal as well. This is usually subtle, but sometimes outright. It is not uncommon to come across this, even in a "Christian" romance novel. Then the reader, once she realizes it's more than she planned on reading, must make a choice: to continue reading or to stop. If a single person happens to be struggling in the first place, this likely will intensify the struggle. *Walk in the Spirit, and ye shall not fulfill the lust of the flesh. For the flesh lusteth against the Spirit, and the Spirit against the flesh: and these are contrary the one to the other* (Gal. 5:16-17) (Also see Gal. 5:25, Romans 8:5, 13:14).

3. Perhaps reason enough is simply that they are fiction. *When I was a child, I spake as a child, I understood as a child, I thought as a child: but when I became a man, I put away childish things.* (1 Cor. 13:11). *Whatsoever things are true...think on these things.* (Phil. 4:8).

4. They are addicting. How many books have you read lately? How late at night do you stay up reading? Do you reach for other books with more desire than for the Bible? If so, where is your first love? Do you hurry through your daily Bible reading, treating the Word as if it's just a task that must be done, so you can spend the rest of your free time reading a novel? When our flesh is being fed, the books of this world tend to be "easier" reading and more captivating than the Bible. *All things are lawful unto me, but all things are not expedient: all things are lawful for me, but I will not be brought under the power of any* (1Cor. 6:12). (Also see Ps. 19:13.)

5. Do you put away your books when you know someone is coming over to visit? *For there is nothing covered, that shall not be revealed; neither hid, that shall not be known* (Luke 12:2). Would you feel comfortable leaving them set out in the open for everyone to see? What if Jesus Himself came to your house to visit you? Yet He already knows what you are reading. Does it glorify Him? Would you be ashamed to read *any* paragraph aloud to your family, your brethren, your minister, or to a friend of the truth? Would doing so cause your light to be dimmed?

6. We are called to holiness and instructed to redeem the time. *See then that ye walk circumspectly, not as fools, but as wise, redeeming the time, because the days are evil* (Eph. 5:15-16). Perhaps you feel the books you read are "not that bad." However, what about if there are "just a few" questionable spots? (1 Cor. 5:6) Even if one could conclude that fiction/romance books were honorable, are there not more edifying ways for a believer to spend his/her time (1 Cor. 10:23)?

Steps to Overcoming

1. The first step is to stop making excuses and justifying your actions, and acknowledging that there is a problem (Ps. 32:5). Recognize that it is Satan who is trying to steal away your thoughts and your time. Do not be overconfident and think that it's not a big

deal. One thing can easily lead to the next, and often does. I started out reading books that most people would consider to be very mild. But one author led to another, which led to another. *Wherefore let him that thinketh he standeth take heed lest he fall* (1 Cor. 10:12).

2. Tell someone you are close to that you are struggling. Do not seek consolation in someone equally weak, but rather, in someone who will hold you accountable. *Confess your faults one to another, and pray one for another, that ye may be healed* (James 5:16).

3. Libraries and bookstores are not evil places. But to one with this weakness, it is best to avoid bookstores and libraries altogether while you are in the heat of the battle (Prov. 4:14-15, 16:3). I personally know it's an area I am tempted in, and therefore I am just better off not even browsing. We should not be curious to "just take a look" at *any* of the world's allurements.

4. Think of other ways that you can spend your time that God would bless you for. Single sisters, especially ones who live alone, need to seek ways to not become lonely. For example, you could listen to a sermon or call an elderly person. You could write about your struggles in a journal or to a friend. These are things that you can ask God's blessings upon without reservation in your heart. *Pure religion and undefiled before God and the Father is this, To visit the fatherless and widows in their affliction, and to keep himself unspotted from the world* (James 1:27). (Also see Eph. 5:15-16; Gal. 6:9.)

Children's books

Many children, like adults, enjoy reading. We like to see our children enjoy books, as it can be an edifying pastime. However, we need to teach our children moderation, because reading can become excessive and lead to problems such as laziness. *Even a child is known by his doings, whether his work be pure, and whether it be right* (Prov. 20:11). (Also see Prov. 22:6.) As children get older, it may become more and more difficult to find decent books for children to read. Comic books that exemplify violence should be strongly discouraged, as well as comic books putting heavy emphasis on sensual boy-girl relationships (such as Archie). I grew up reading Archie comic books, and I can tell you from experience it was counterproductive to biblical training. Your children's attitudes will be influenced by what they read! There *are* good books out there for pre-teens and teens. It is worth the effort to find wholesome books. Ask other parents or teachers for recommendations. *Keep thy heart with all diligence; for out of it are the issues of life* (Prov. 4:23).

Conclusion

I beseech you therefore, brethren, by the mercies of God, that ye present your bodies a living sacrifice, holy, acceptable unto God, which is your reasonable service. And be not conformed to this world: but be ye transformed by the renewing of your mind, that ye may prove what is that good, and acceptable, and perfect, will of God (Romans 12:1-2).

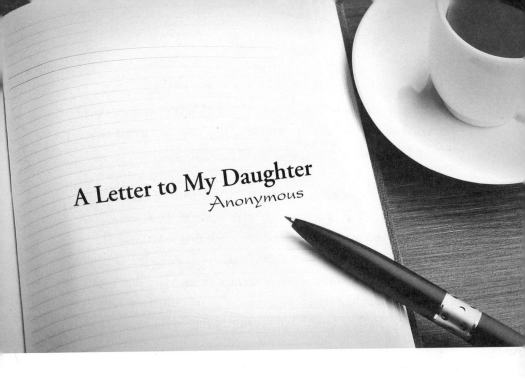

A Letter to My Daughter

Anonymous

You have just arrived home from church. You come into your bedroom and put your Bible on the dresser. Suddenly you hear a noise in your closet. You open the closet door to investigate. Immediately a hand grips your arm and a gruff voice growls, "Gotcha!" You go from pale to pink to purple to pale. Your nervous system automatically kicks in, releasing adrenaline into your bloodstream. Your heart races. Your blood pressure rises. You let out a blood-curdling scream.

Did you intend to do all this when you first came into the bedroom? Why didn't you control your emotions? Is it right for you to react so out of control? Should godly Christian women not have their emotions in control at all times?

I ask you that because many an honest (and maybe a tad naive) woman has asked, "If a Christian man sees a partially exposed woman and has a problem with that, is that not a sign that he is perverted?"

Yes, he is perverted. We all are. There used to be a time at the beginning of time when an all-wise Creator made man and woman perfect. And naked. The Bible says: *And they were both naked, the man and his wife, and were not ashamed* (Genesis 2:25).

That whole picture changed. After the woman partook of the fruit and gave to her husband, they went looking for something to cover their nakedness because they were ashamed. Here the all-wise Creator stepped in and did something about that nakedness. He covered them both. He covered their nakedness. From this we can gather that if God clothed both of them, it is necessary that both man and woman be covered. Not because all of a sudden something had changed in their bodies, but because of the sin they now had to deal with. Sin opened their eyes to nakedness.

Clothing helps control the sinful nature. Satan tries to pervert all things God made. It is not that beauty is perversion. It just has to be covered so there is no perversion.

But even though we are perverted, that is not the first thing that kicks in when a man sees parts of a woman that should be covered. It is the automatic nervous system that kicks in and reacts. It cannot be helped, just the same as you could not help the reaction when that hand grabbed your arm. Just because you, as a woman, do not experience that reaction, does not mean it does not happen. Men are aroused by sight. Extremely so! Sure, a Christian man can, and needs to, look away, resist the devil, and think on other things. But that does not reverse what already happened!

As my daughter, I want you to know this and the rest of what I want to share with you. It will keep you pure. It will protect you. It will make you wise.

We live in a society that revels in nakedness. We are bombarded with it on billboards, magazines, the daily paper, and women on the street. Sadly, many naive Christian women have copied some of the trends of this nakedness and gone up for public display. So, not only do we as men have to be resisting the devil on the street, we have to do it in church too. Again, as a woman you may not understand it, but it is true. It is not only the weak who struggle with this. It is a natural thing given to men by an all-wise Creator, intending for a beautiful relationship between a man and his wife!

Men were created to be initiators. Women were created to be responders. Any woman in a marriage relationship can be thankful for the stimulation the female body evokes in a man. No woman is perfect in body, but *all* women have enough to stimulate a man. Exactly how God intended it to be! But that is also why *all* females have to be so careful in the way they dress, walk, bend over, or act.

The more "right" your figure is, the more careful you have to be. And you are a poor judge as to what is "right." Those breasts or hips that you think are "too big" or "too gross," and positively hate, may be the very things that will turn on a man. And how beautiful, if that is the man's wife. But what if she isn't? She becomes a snare and a fiery dart in the hand of Satan. And if you are small…? You are still female. A small woman may be able to hide her figure a little bit easier, but that doesn't mean she may not be stimulating to a man's eye.

And I repeat: The feminine shape is beautiful! Both in the eyes of the Creator who made you that way and in the eyes of *all* men. That is why you have to cover it so not *all* men see it.

In order for you to have no doubt as to what I am speaking about, let me specifically explain a few areas in which you have to be careful. I am writing this so you can have something to read and reread; something to supplement what we have already taught you. I am not trying to be legalistic or pushy in what I say. I am trying to protect your purity. I do not want you to be an accessory in the devil's arsenal. I do not want you to be a Bathsheba.

Bathsheba had no intention to make anyone sin. All she was doing was bathing in a place where she was visible. And David was not wicked either. The Bible says he was a man after God's own heart (Acts 13:22). But in the presence of a naked woman, he was weak. She started a process that ended up in sin, murder, and much heartache. It would not have happened if she would have bathed in a secluded place.

You say, "I only bathe in a secluded place." I commend you for that and I will always strive to provide you with just such a place. But the sin of Bathsheba was exposure of skin that should not have been public. When we make other people sin, we are accountable for that. The Bible says, *Neither be partaker of other men's sins: keep thyself pure* (1 Timothy 5:22). The woman who does not practice modesty becomes a participant in the sins of the men who lust for her. Because of this the Scriptures insist that a woman be modest.

The following points are some ways in which you can expose too much of yourself:

SHORT DRESSES

What is short? That is a question many women ask. Let me just tell you that legs can be very seductive. The more exposed they are, the more seductive. Why? Because it draws the eyes and the imagination *up* the legs. In order to not tempt the average man you will have to have your dresses as long as possible. Remember that even if a dress comes well below the knees when you are standing, it will come up further when you sit down. And do not think only of the front part *you* see. Many a woman sits and spreads her skirts around the front and forgets that the back is exposed to full view.

SHORT SLEEVES

Again, what is short? If you know men have a problem with exposed skin, how much do you want to expose? A meek woman will cover instead of trying to see how much she can expose. A general rule is that at least from the elbow up it should be covered.

TIGHT CLOTHES

Women think that because they have their skin covered, they are no longer naked. That is far from true. If the clothing you wear reveals the shape of your breasts and the contour of your hips, in a sinful man's eye it really is not much different than the bare skin. Sure, his automatic nervous system will probably not react quite as fast, but it still will.

As I said before, most women have some kind of flaw. If it is covered with tight clothing that reveals the shape, the flaw is gone, but the shape is still there.

LOW NECKLINES

Low necklines expose skin and draw the eye to the neck and the breasts. The more you reveal, the more "loose" you look. You are saying, "Look at this." If you expose those parts, a man's eye will constantly be drawn to them. I have heard some women gripe about how men look at their chests instead of their eyes when they talk. It could be your fault if you wear low necklines.

THIN AND CLINGY FABRICS

Thin and clingy fabrics fall in the same category as tight clothes because they *reveal*. Partial nudity can have a stronger allure than total nudity simply because it awakens and stimulates the imagination. Partial nudity calls for a closer look to finish the picture. Fashion designers know all about this. That is why they use semitransparent and clingy fabrics to achieve the effect.

As a child of God you will want to avoid all fabrics that draw attention to your body instead of to Christ. In selecting fabrics you will need to keep in mind that other people will see you in all positions and from all angles. A fabric that is not thick enough will allow the shape to be seen if there is a strong backlight. Example: When you stand in a doorway.

You will also need to keep in mind that the wind blows. A thin and clingy fabric will mold to your body and reveal your figure.

Any fabric that shows the shape or shade of undergarments is too thin or clingy. And if it just about shows when you are standing, what will it do when you bend over or squat to talk to a child? Which brings me to my next point:

POSTURE AND BODY LANGUAGE

You can cover yourself ever so carefully but ruin the whole effect with posture. In the presence of others, *never* bend over at your waist. Rather, bend your knees. Experiment in front of a mirror or get someone to help you. The difference is astounding.

Many women also forget to sit correctly. Make sure that every time you sit, your dress is not tight over your hips or legs. Also, do not sit on the floor with your legs wide open. Even if you make sure you are covered, the position is sensual to some men.

How do you walk? A Christian lady will *never* want to walk with her chest pushed out or with hips swinging. It draws attention to two striking features on a woman's anatomy. High heels tend to bring out these two features, so a Christian woman will avoid high heels at all costs.

Another thing to remember is that modesty also has to do with the way you carry yourself, the way you smile, and what you do with your eyes. Make sure you have a *meek (humble, modest, mild) and quiet (tempered, docile, serene, calm) spirit* (1 Peter 3:4).

Hair Arrangements

Ever notice how hair is one thing many women spend a lot of time with? It is because men also like hair. Not all men are affected by hair in the same way. And some men are hardly affected at all. But, hair is a glory to the woman (1 Corinthians 11:15). When that "glory" is exposed, it can turn men on. Even a sensual little wisp, if that is that man's weakness. Therefore, be sure the glory of your hair is covered and you are not fixing your hair to be noticed.

Accessories

Be *very* sure that your choice of footwear, watches, purses, etc. are not to draw attention to *you*. These things make statements about who you are. If you think you have to have matching and color-coordinated accessories, or have to have a different pair for each occasion, rest assured it is *not* something that was prompted by the Holy Spirit, or a meek and quiet spirit in you.

The spirit of 1 Peter 3:4 will eliminate all such things as colors, dyes, and nail polish. Also the amount and kind of perfumes. Now, do not misunderstand me. I am not banning perfumes. They are *very* necessary for a lot of us to cut down body odors. But an excess of perfume many times stimulates sensuality. Why would a modest and tempered woman use an excess of perfume? Is it not to be noticed, or to make a statement?

oooooooooooooooooooooooooooooooooooooooooooooooooooooooooooooooooooooooooooo

There is a direct relation between nudity and sexual immorality. On the other hand, there are plenty of men out there who will imagine what they cannot even see. That is *their* problem. Just make sure *you* are not triggering it.

Not all men are created equal. Something that triggers one man might not arouse another. You do not know what that might be. Therefore, keep that feminine beauty covered. In 1 Peter 3:1-6 we find that the Christian woman should not stress the outward beauty, rather the inner beauty. If you exhibit the outer beauty, few men will even try or be able to look for the inner beauty.

Are you afraid of men by now? You should not have to be if you follow the spirit of these guidelines, remain open to the promptings of the Holy Spirit, communicate with us and other mature people about this, keep a meek and quiet spirit, and associate with the proper men. If you do this you will gain the respect of *all* men and also be a delight to Christian men who will be very thankful for a safe haven for their eyes. Best of all, God will be glorified!

Your Dad

Recognizing Families of Incest
Anonymous

One way we can understand, explain, and prevent the sexual abuse of children is to take an honest look at the families where incest (sexual abuse within the family) has been reported. There are a number of factors that help us understand the family of the child victim of incest. They are:

1. What is the distribution of power and control among members?

2. What is the degree of family isolation, physically, emotionally, and socially?

3. To what degree are boundaries and respectful limits blurred among members?

4. Is there a balance of independence versus dependence among the adults and children?

5. What is the environment of the home in regards to sleeping quarters and bathrooms?

6. Do the parents have a poor marriage relationship?

7. Are ultra strict guidance and discipline measures used?

8. Does the family communicate well?

9. How intimate is the family?

10. Does the family have a negative view regarding children and childhood?

No two families experiencing incest are exactly alike, but they often have some common ground.

In many families where incest occurs the father of the home has complete control over the entire household, including the mother. The mother is treated like one of the children, or maybe only a little better than a child. This family system provides poor examples of adult behavior to the children. All of the more powerful members of the family system can be expected to exert power over the weaker members in ways that ignore the needs of the less powerful, especially the children. Older brothers may come to believe that it is their right to use their sisters sexually if they wish. If the father uses this power to use one of the children to meet his sexual needs, the child is powerless to exert herself. There are no lines of communication open for the child to turn to for help in this difficult situation. Help for the child victim will have to come from some outside source.

Families that experience incest are often isolated in one or more ways. Often one or both parents feels that the world is a hostile, cold, and uncaring place and therefore separate themselves from others. They will often isolate themselves from normal social functions and contacts and look to the family unit to fulfill all their needs, including their sexual needs. This will be enforced by one or both of the parents who feel insecure and needy. You will find this happening both in the families that exert power and those that are isolated. Mothers that are not having their emotional needs met by their husbands or other outside contacts will turn to their own children, often their sons, and the emotional dependency can turn sexual.

Respectful boundaries are not known or practiced in families where incest is happening. Having healthy boundaries is an important part of feeling independent, safe, and respected. This includes physical boundaries and emotional boundaries. If there are unhealthy emotional boundaries there is a role reversal and children are expected to meet the needs of their parents or older children. When these normal boundaries are blurred, children are not allowed to say "no" to a parent under any circumstances, including keeping their private body parts from misuse. When physical boundaries are blurred, children of opposite sexes may share sleeping space regardless of their ages and there will be no rules about appropriate touching.

There will be no healthy independence of the family members; instead families experiencing incest may encourage dependence. Dependence keeps up the misuse of power and control and sends the message that one person's needs should be met even at the expense of another. Those with more power in the family teach the lesson that it is okay to take from others rather than sharing or giving.

When the abuser is a parent, the abuse often causes a complete breakdown of the marriage relationship. However, many couples maintain a false image of their relationship, both in public and inside the family. This is one reason that people are often shocked when the incest is disclosed. This deception is confusing for the children who learn that life patterns are built on lies. In most families of abusers, everyone suspects or knows that something is wrong, but no one really knows what the problem is. It is the big family secret.

In many abusive homes parents are inflexible and controlling in the ways they discipline their children. Children learn that there is a serious price to pay for saying "no." This sets the stage for the child not being able to say "no" to abuse either.

True intimacy is built on trust, commitment, honesty, and openness in communication. In incest homes, there is an emptiness where intimacy should be. This can lead the older children of the family to commit incest out of anger, feelings of rejection, inadequacy, or abandonment.

The communication patterns in abusive families are dishonest and unhealthy. They will keep certain subjects completely off limits and use blaming and misinformation. There will be the family secrets and lies. There will be honest feelings, needs, rules, beliefs, and hopes at the heart of every healthy family communication.

Careful observance by other members of the church or community may be the only way that help will arrive for these sad situations. The observing members will want to notify a church leader or contact children's services directly to start the process of holding the abuser responsible and bringing safety and healing for the abused child. It must be recognized that even if the abuse does not directly affect one's own family, anyone that finds out about or becomes suspicious of such things is responsible to do something about it. Abusers are rarely satisfied with abusing only one person, and in reporting abuse we are in the long run protecting our own children. Since the abused often become abusers, by reporting and discontinuing abuse we may be protecting our own children for many more years to come, and we may be protecting our future grandchildren. Be willing to report. Be willing to go for help. Be willing to protect an innocent child.

The
Spirit
of
Fear

Anonymous

I have never been sexually abused, but I've had family members who were, so I've seen some of the physical, emotional, and spiritual consequences of abuse. They can be devastating.

Even before I was married, I wondered how parents can raise pure children in a perverted world. It seemed impossible because evil is thrown at us every time we step outside our homes. It even lurks in our so-called Christian circles. A a small seed of fear took root in my heart.

Eventually I got married to a wonderful, godly man and in time, God blessed us with children. I held my children, glad for their smallness, their innocence. And I struggled with the question. *How can we lead our children…?* Fear thrust up hardy, green shoots.

We grew more aware of the perversion of this world. Satan bombarded us from the outside. Evil entered our home in the form of phone calls and junk mail. And we had wanted our homes to be a safe place for our children.

But we discovered that the worst attacks come from within. Family gatherings became difficult. Some families allow children play unsupervised for hours. There were no limits or guidelines on proper boy/girl contact. Immorality among their children is considered wrong, of course and punished. But they seem detached. "It's all part of the Adamic nature children are born with," one mother told me. "They must just learn to control it as they grow up." And their children still run around unsupervised.

Fear's heavy footsteps tramped beside me. It smothered our children, because I would not let them out of my sight at family gatherings, and they complained because they couldn't play with the others. Fear threatened to overwhelm us.

In desperation we fall to our knees and cry for help. Jesus came, and He showed us that fear must go, or it will destroy our family. We know what fear does. It causes us to panic the minute our child disappears at a family gathering. When several of the children spent time behind locked doors, we immediately assume the worst.

Fear caused us to shun other family members because we are afraid their children abuse ours. It causes us to lose sleep at night, and even worse, to lose out spiritually. It damages relationships.

We see the effects of fear in the lives of others who were trying to protect their children. One mother who had been abused herself spanked her one-year-old daughter whenever her dress went a few inches above her ankles. This little girl is two now, and goes around telling other little girls (and their mothers) to pull their dresses further down. This same little girl lives with fear unlike any I've ever seen in a child.

"Fear leads us away from God." We recognized that truth at last. Why? Because God has not given us the spirit of fear; but of power, and of love, and of a sound mind.

God gives us faith. Faith is the opposite of fear. It is believing that what God says is true. Faith helped us to see that fear is a stronghold that must be pulled down. Faith urges us to be accountable for fear, repent from it and renounce it. Through faith we receive the Holy Spirit, Jesus, and our heavenly Father into our hearts, and surrender every thing into His care.

We surrender our children.

Through faith we see the need for further purity in our own lives. As we deal with these issues, He shows us how to teach our children to lead pure and holy lives.

We pray that God will protect the moral purity of our children. But faith also gives us courage to set guidelines for our children without smothering them. We take responsibility to check up on them, and we never let them congregate behind locked doors or in barns. At times we must sacrifice adult conversation and help the children play. They love it and we are right there with them and know what is going on.

Our faith also gives us love for our brethren who disagree with us about these subjects. We try to speak the truth in love. We do not want to condemn.

As we learn more of the Almighty God through faith, He gives us wisdom to teach our children about purity in an honest, matter-of-fact way. He helps us walk the narrow road between the two ditches—the ditch of no teaching and the ditch of over teaching. One is as harmful as the other.

We are young parents, just starting on this road. We shrink at times from the monster of fear, when he leaps from the ditch to pull us in. But, praise the Lord, we have found protection in the shield of faith. We hold it high and with our eyes on Jesus, we march onward, upward, leading our children to Him.

Preventing Sexual Abuse in Schools
-A Plea to Teachers

Marvin Wengerd

As a teacher you have a great responsibility to protect young children from abuse. Here are things to watch for and avoid that will make your school safer.

1. Disrespect. Abuse rarely happens where respect that a boy should have for girls has not broken down. Are boys being too familiar? Mocking? Critical? Restore respect as quickly as possible.

2. Inappropriate touching. Fondling is the second stage of abuse. Are boys touching girls inappropriately? Do they push girls around? Avoid games where touching is part of the game—especially for upper graders. As a teacher you need to avoid inappropriate physical contact with your students. Your upper graders have an emerging awareness of sexuality and are stimulated quickly.

3. Don't tolerate boy/girl teasing. Explain the sacredness of romantic relationships and how all of this needs to wait until the right time.

4. Never speak lightly of sexual things to any student. Watch for

conversations that include details about animal reproduction. If the subject comes up, quickly make it clear that this is not a subject appropriate for school. Avoid acting like it is dirty or naughty. School is just not the right place.

5. Listen for bathroom talk and end all discussions that include it. Discussion of body parts and body functions that are not part of a health curriculum should be avoided.

6. Books. Some parents are careless of the reading material of older siblings. These have a way of coming into the school. Make it clear that romance books and books with explicit scenes are not to be in school. Ask your board's help if needed.

7. Monitor restrooms. Restrooms are the natural place for wrong sexual things to occur. As a girl teacher you should enter the boys' restroom only in an emergency, but if you perceive an emergency you have the responsibility to do so. Speak to your students about appropriate and inappropriate restroom behavior. Get help from your board and parents immediately if you sense sexual aggression occurring in restrooms. Never allow older boys to prey on younger boys in the restroom. Be aggressive with ending any activity that scars a child.

8. Report any inappropriate sexual behavior between your co-teacher and students. Be alert for lack of respect, not keeping appropriate distance, touching, and/or careless or inappropriate sexual talk between teachers and students. Again, be fairly aggressive instead of having a passive attitude. Involve authority immediately. Don't wait until the school year is over to speak up.

RESOURCES

Resources from Christian Light Publications, PO Box 1212, Harrisonburg, VA 22803, 540.434.0763

Living a Pure Life—A practical guide to understanding sexual sin and biblical answers for breaking sin's power, by John Coblentz

God's Will for My Body—Guidance for adolescents, by John Coblentz

God's Will for Love in Marriage—Cultivating marital intimacy, by John Coblentz

Looking at Myself Before Loving Someone Else—A workbook to prepare young people for godly courtship by, John Coblentz

Beauty for Ashes—Biblical help for the sexually abused, by John Coblentz

---

Sacred Subjects—7 booklets to help you talk about sacred things to your child. Pathway Publishers, 43632 County Rd 390, Bloomingdale, MI 49026

A Trampled Flower Can Rise Again—From the pain of abuse to healing in Christ, by Lena M Martin, Book Centra, 2673 TR 421, Sugarcreek, OH 44681, 877.442.6657

When Trust Is Lost—Healing for victims of sexual abuse, RBC Ministries, PO Box 2222, Grand Rapids, MI 49501

Protecting Your Children from Abuse—A guide to parents who care about their little ones, by Mary Ann Brechbill, 2373 St Thomas-Edenville Road, Chambersburg, PA 17202, 717.369.5185

3.00